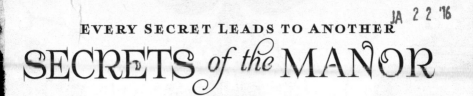

EVERY SECRET LEADS TO ANOTHER

# SECRETS *of the* MANOR

Camille's Story, 1910

BY

## ADELE WHITBY

Simon Spotlight

New York   London   Toronto   Sydney   New Delhi

SIMON SPOTLIGHT
An imprint of Simon & Schuster Children's Publishing Division
1230 Avenue of the Americas, New York, New York 10020
This Simon Spotlight hardcover edition May 2015
Copyright © 2015 by Simon & Schuster, Inc. Text by Ellie O'Ryan.
Cover illustrations by Francesca Resta. Interior illustrations by Jaime Zollars.
All rights reserved, including the right of reproduction in whole or in part in any form. SIMON SPOTLIGHT and colophon are registered trademarks of Simon & Schuster, Inc. For information about special discounts for bulk purchases, please contact Simon & Schuster Special Sales at 1-866-506-1949 or business@simonandschuster.com.
Designed by Laura Roode. The text of this book was set in Adobe Caslon Pro.
Manufactured in the United States of America 0415 FFG
2 4 6 8 10 9 7 5 3 1
ISBN 978-1-4814-3989-3 (hc)
ISBN 978-1-4814-3988-6 (pbk)
ISBN 978-1-4814-3990-9 (eBook)
Library of Congress Control Number
2014947118

I stared into the pot as the water began to boil, melting the knob of butter into a shiny yellow slick. "Now?" I asked anxiously. "Should I add the flour now?"

Across the kitchen, Mama was whisking egg whites at a furious pace. "Is the butter melted, Camille?" she called.

"Almost," I replied. "Almost . . . yes!"

"Good. Now add the flour all at once and stir as hard as you can. Mind the stove, now. I don't want you to burn yourself again."

"All at once?" I repeated.

"Yes. Just pour it in and begin stirring. Don't stop until it's come together in a thick dough."

"Yes, Mama."

I bit my tongue as I reached for the flour; Mama had helped me measure just the right amount. *All at once,* I reminded myself. Then I poured the flour into the pot. But I must've poured it a bit *too* fast, because a huge cloud of the stuff rose into the air!

"Oh!" I cried, rubbing my powdery face. *"Ah-ah-ahhhh-choo!"*

The scullery maids started to giggle—and who could blame them? My shenanigans at the stove were a constant source of entertainment for the entire kitchen staff. But I knew that they didn't mean any harm by their laughter. After all, I'm sure I made a funny picture, now that my dark, chestnut-brown hair was as white as a powdered wig!

"Are you all right, Camille?" Mama said.

"Yes, Mama. I'm fine," I replied as I tried not to sneeze again. I focused all my attention on stirring, stirring, stirring the gooey mix in the pot. Mama was trained as a pastry chef by her father, Alistair Beaudin, a famous chef who was known throughout all of France for his delicious desserts. The Beaudin family method for making light, delicate profiteroles was a carefully guarded secret, and just one of the reasons why Monsieur Henri and Madame Colette Rousseau had been so eager to hire Mama when she had finished her apprenticeship. Mama had been just as eager to accept their offer of employment, since she and my father, the groundskeeper at Rousseau Manor, were engaged to be married. Monsieur Henri used to joke about what a perfect match it was, bringing together two sweethearts and satisfying his sweet tooth at the same time. But he had stopped making that joke after Papa died.

Mama and I still missed Papa terribly, but Monsieur Henri and Madame Colette had done everything in their power to ease our pain. Since they had no children, the Rousseaus had dedicated their ample time and fortune to helping others, including Mama and me. Just after Papa's death, the Rousseaus had promised that they would always take care of us, no matter what. And in keeping that promise, they had earned our loyalty—for life. It was a privilege to work at Rousseau Manor, one of the grandest homes in all of France. The manor, and the estate it sat on, had been in the Rousseau family for generations. Ever since my tenth birthday almost two years ago, Mama had been trying her best to train me in the pastry arts so that I, too, could carry on the Beaudin family tradition. But despite my heritage, I was a disaster in the kitchen! Somehow, though, Mama had limitless patience with me. And if she wouldn't give up, then I wouldn't either.

I stirred and stirred until my arm began to ache. Then, like magic, it happened: The sticky flour and buttery water combined to make a smooth, shiny dough.

"Mama!" I cried. "I did it! I did it!"

"Well done, Camille!" she said proudly from across the kitchen, and even the scullery maids began to applaud. I beamed with pleasure.

"Now what?" I asked.

"Let it rest for a few minutes to cool," Mama told me. "Then you can add the eggs, one at a time. Twelve ought to do it. Remember to beat well after each addition, Camille. And don't add them too soon, or else the heat from the dough will cook them."

"I won't," I promised. Then I ducked into the pantry for the eggs I'd gathered. Since spring had arrived, the hens had been laying even more eggs than usual; I'd already collected two large baskets and it wasn't even noon! I wouldn't be a bit surprised if Mrs. Plourde, the cook, decided to make a quiche for luncheon.

I held out my apron skirt to make a pouch for the eggs as I counted them, one by one. As I gently placed each egg in my apron skirt, I heard a sharp voice say my

4

name. My heart sank. I knew who it was right away: Bernadette, the head housemaid and one of the most powerful servants at Rousseau Manor. Bernadette was quick to find fault, especially with me. She was always displeased with how I folded the napkins or scoured the pans. Even my thick hair, which resisted all my efforts to stay in a tidy plait, seemed to offend her.

"Camille!" she barked again. "What are you doing?"

"I was—"

"Dawdling, most likely." She spoke over me with a contemptuous sniff. "As if there wasn't enough work to be done around here."

"But—"

"No excuses," Bernadette said as she grabbed hold of my elbow and escorted me back to the kitchen. "Now, show me your task, or I'll send you off to polish the silver."

"I'm making dough for the profiteroles," I tried to explain as I carefully placed the eggs in a bowl. "There's croquembouche on the menu tonight."

"Croquembouche?" Bernadette asked. She raised an eyebrow in disbelief. "And your mother trusted *you* with the profiteroles?"

I nodded miserably. It was no secret that croquem-bouche, a tall tower made of airy profiteroles filled with creamy custard and held in place by a sticky caramel sauce, was one of the most challenging desserts to make. Even I had to wonder what Mama was thinking when she asked for my help.

"Then you'd best get on with it," said Bernadette. She folded her bony arms across her chest, and I could tell that she intended to watch every single thing I did.

*What if the dough is still too hot?* I worried. I snuck a glance around the kitchen, but Mama must have stepped out.

"Get on with it, I said," Bernadette snapped.

I touched the side of the pot. It still felt warm ... but was it *too* warm? Oh, how I wished that Mama would return! But one look at Bernadette's stern face told me that I didn't dare delay. I took a deep breath and cracked an egg as carefully as I could. Even so, a fragment of the shell tumbled into the pot. I reached in quickly to retrieve it, hoping that Bernadette wouldn't notice. But she did, of course. She noticed everything.

"I cannot imagine that Monsieur Henri wishes to eat eggshells in his croquembouche," she said pointedly.

6

"No," I murmured as I began to whisk the egg into the dough.

I focused all my attention on the mound of dough. With each stir, the egg should've disappeared more and more—but instead it began to clump together. My heart sank. It was obvious even to me that I'd made a mistake and added the egg too soon.

Bernadette peered into the pot. "Well, now it's gone and curdled," she told me. "You've ruined it."

Just then, thankfully, Mama returned to the kitchen. As she hurried over to us, there was hardly a trace of the limp she had from breaking her ankle last winter, but I knew Mama did everything in her power to conceal the truth: Most days her ankle hurt more than she wanted to admit.

"Ahh, Bernadette, how nice to see you," she said. "Thank you for helping Camille while I was away."

"Really, Marie, I can't imagine what you were thinking when you let her make the profiteroles," Bernadette said, shaking her head in disgust. "Just look at this slop! It's hardly fit for the pigs."

A slight frown crossed Mama's face as she looked into the pot. "The mixture was still too hot for the egg," she remarked. "It needed more time to cool."

*Oh, Mama, I didn't* want *to add it!* I longed to say—but I knew I had to hold my tongue. Mama must have seen the tears in my eyes because she continued in a very cheerful voice. "It's no harm. We can start over."

"A waste of food." Bernadette sniffed. "Camille is not experienced enough for a task like this."

"It is true that Camille is young," Mama replied. "But I am confident that she will learn by doing. She tries very hard, you know."

"Indeed, she does!" We all turned around to see that Madame Colette had entered the kitchen. She looked beautiful, as always, with her silver hair twisted into a soft chignon at the base of her neck. Bernadette, Mama, and I all curtsied at once.

"My goodness, Camille, look at you!" continued Madame Colette. "The flour on your face is enough to show me how hard you've been working today."

"Thank you, madame," I said with a curtsy as Mama passed me a damp cloth to clean my face.

Madame Colette glanced into the pot, but if she was dismayed to see the mess inside it, she didn't show it. "Henri is truly looking forward to tonight's dessert," she said kindly. "And I know he will be even more pleased to learn that Camille helped make it. Now, Bernadette, did you need to see me?"

"Yes, madame, and thank you for your time," Bernadette replied as she led Madame Colette to her office across the hall. As soon as they were gone, I breathed a sigh of relief.

"I am so sorry, Mama," I said, gesturing to the mess in the pot. "I wanted to wait, but Bernadette—"

Mama shook her head. "No apologies necessary, Camille," she said in a gentle voice, but I could see that she was upset. "I can imagine what happened. It's no trouble to start again. Do you remember what to do?"

"Yes."

"Then go ahead and get started. You'll do fine," Mama said with an encouraging smile. She picked up the pot. "I'll take this out to the pigs."

As I began to measure more water into another pot, I realized that Bernadette had left her office door open. I could clearly hear every word of her conversation with Madame Colette. *How odd*, I thought. *Bernadette* always *shuts her door.*

I tried not to eavesdrop, but it was impossible to

ignore them as they chatted about Rousseau Manor's staffing needs. Then Bernadette said something that caught my attention.

"I am afraid, madame, that I must ask of you a very special favor."

"Of course, Bernadette," Madame Colette replied. "You may go ahead."

"It is about my cousin, Philippe Archambault," Bernadette continued. "He and his family lived near the river before the flood. They lost . . . everything."

Madame Colette said nothing, but I could picture the look of concern that had surely crossed her face. All through last summer and fall, into the winter, the rain had poured—more rain than anyone could remember falling before. By the time January arrived, bringing with it even more rainstorms, the River Seine had begun to rise. The sodden ground could hold no more water, and it oozed up through pipes and drains, until nearly all of Paris was flooded. In some places, all that could be seen were the tops of the trees! It was a slow flood; the muddy water rose with the pace of molasses, providing enough time for most Parisians to escape to higher, dryer ground.

To many people who lived on country estates at the edges of the city, the flood was a marvelous spectacle to gawk at. They traveled to the heart of Paris just to see the buildings underwater, the rickety bridges that supported daring escapes, and the fireboats sailing down streets where horses used to pull buggies alongside clattering automobiles. The Rousseaus, however, would never be so coarse as to enjoy the misfortune of others. At news of the first survivors to escape from the flooded city, they had opened the doors of Rousseau Manor, welcoming as many people as the servants' quarters could hold. Yes, it was crowded; yes, the workload had never been greater (especially for those of us in the kitchen); but I couldn't have been more proud of Monsieur Henri and Madame Colette. Their generous spirits were an inspiration to us all.

"How can I help?" Madame Colette asked Bernadette.

"Might there . . . be room for them here?"

"I would love to offer them our hospitality, of course," Madame Colette said right away. "But we are already filled to capacity." She sighed heavily. "How many? Your cousin and his wife?"

"Yes. And their two children. Please, madame, they have been living in a church—"

"Bernadette, you need not plead their case to me. I have the greatest sympathy for those who lost everything to the flood waters," Madame Colette interrupted gently. "But I don't know where we could house an entire family."

"What about the groundskeeper's cottage?" Bernadette suggested.

I clapped my hand over my mouth in surprise. The groundskeeper's cottage? That was where Mama and I lived! Of course I knew it was a luxury—a true indulgence—that the Rousseaus had allowed us to stay there even after Papa died. And I knew that we had no right to expect such wonderful accommodations— a cheerful two-bedroom cottage with its very own kitchen, separate from the manor, when the rest of the staff shared rooms in the attic.

But that little cottage was our home. It was the only home I had ever known.

Just then Mama returned from the courtyard. "Camille, I—" she began to say. But I held a finger to my lips before she could continue.

"The estate needs a full-time groundskeeper again, madame," Bernadette pressed. "It has been too long. Marcel tries his best, but he comes only twice a week. The neglect of the gardens and the orchards has begun to show. My cousin Philippe would be honored to tend them. He would care for these grounds as if they were his very own. And his son is nearly full-grown! If you bring them to Rousseau Manor, it would be like hiring *two* groundskeepers."

"I see."

"Not to mention, his wife, Élise, is a fine cook. She has even worked in a restaurant." Bernadette continued earnestly. "She would welcome the chance to serve in the kitchens. Why, perhaps Élise could be responsible for cooking meals for the staff! We both know that the kitchen staff has been terribly taxed by preparing all the additional meals for our guests. And Philippe's daughter is as sweet as could be. I tell you, madame, that my cousin and his family would prove themselves to be a great asset here. Any kindness you showed them would be repaid many times over."

There was a long pause.

13

"Please," Bernadette finally said. "I never ask for special consideration, madame. But this is my family. My flesh and blood. I cannot bear to think of them spending one more night on the streets—"

"Of course, Bernadette. Say no more," Madame Colette interrupted her. "Please tell your cousin that he is welcome at Rousseau Manor, and I am sure that he will make a fine groundskeeper. You're right. It *has* been too long."

"And the cottage?"

"Yes," Madame Colette replied. "They will be able to move in shortly. I hope they will find it quite comfortable."

Bernadette did not respond. Or perhaps she did and I couldn't hear her because I was so stunned that nothing else mattered in that moment: not the daunting croquembouche waiting to be made; not the pigs outside, gleefully eating the dough I'd ruined; and not the flour that had drifted out of my hair and into my eyes, making them smart. No, there was only one thing I could think about in that moment:

Where were Mama and I going to live?

*M*ama—" I whispered.

She smiled reassuringly at me. "It will be all right, Camille," she said. "You mustn't worry."

"But—"

"The Rousseaus promised that they would always look out for us," she continued. "And they always have."

I tried to smile back at her, but it wasn't easy. Mama didn't seem a bit concerned, but was she just trying to protect me? I didn't much care if we moved to the servants' quarters—but what about *her*? How would she ever manage to climb four steep, narrow flights of stairs to reach her room in the attic, with her ankle still swollen and tender by the time she finished her work each night?

"Goodness, Camille, that's about to boil over," Mama said suddenly.

"Sorry!" I exclaimed. *Pay attention!* I told myself.

I couldn't afford another mishap in the kitchen, especially since I had a feeling that Bernadette would be back any moment, watching—and waiting—for me to make a mistake.

"Go ahead and add the flour, dear one," Mama said.

This time, I was much more careful, adding the flour in a slow pour so that none of it billowed outside the pot. I stirred it vigorously, wondering all the while when Bernadette would return. When she did, she wasn't alone; Madame Colette accompanied her.

"I do hate to interrupt you, but I should like to see you and Camille in my parlor at your earliest convenience," Madame Colette said to Mama.

*This is it,* I thought, my heart pounding. Behind Madame Colette, I was surprised to see an unkind smile on Bernadette's face. She almost looked triumphant! But I must've been mistaken. Surely Bernadette was just happy for her cousin, as she should be. I would've been happy for them too, if I weren't so worried about Mama and her ankle. I tried to catch her eye, but she was looking at Madame Colette.

"We can come right now, if it would be convenient,"

Mama said. "The profiterole dough must rest before we can add the eggs."

"Wonderful," Madame Colette replied. "Come with me."

We followed her upstairs to the bright, sun-filled parlor where Madame Colette attended to her daily responsibilities. Even though I was dreading hearing the news directly from Madame Colette, I couldn't help looking forward to sharing a few moments with her. She was truly one of the kindest, most charming people I'd ever met, and she somehow knew how to make everyone feel at ease—from visiting royalty to a simple servant's daughter like me.

"How are you both?" Madame Colette asked once we were seated. "Marie, it is so good to see you up and about again! I trust your ankle is healing nicely?"

"I am feeling quite well, thank you," Mama replied. "Dr. Olivier did a masterful job."

"I hope you will remember to rest whenever you feel the need," Madame Colette told her. "There is no dessert so important that you must suffer to make it."

Then, with a twinkle in her pretty green eyes, Madame Colette leaned toward us and whispered loudly, "Though Henri, of course, might disagree!"

We all shared a laugh then, and I found that the longer I was sitting with Madame Colette, the more reassured I felt. *Mama was right,* I thought. *Madame Colette* will *look after us.*

"It has come to my attention that there is a family, displaced by the flood, that needs a place to stay," Madame Colette continued. "I know that we are filled to capacity already, but when I heard that there were children involved, I didn't see how I could possibly refuse the request. I know that this will come as something of a shock, but I hope you will understand when I tell you that I think it would be best for them to move into the groundskeeper's cottage."

"Of course," Mama said right away. "It is the perfect solution! The cottage will be just the thing for them. Oh, the poor dears—when I think about the children, struggling without a home of their own these past months!"

Madame Colette placed her smooth, white hand over Mama's hand, neatly covering the scars and burns from all Mama's years in the kitchen. "I know, Marie," she said. "The situation tugs at my heart, as well. Thank you for being so understanding."

"It is the *only* thing to do," Mama said. "Camille and I need no special accommodations, madame. We are grateful just to be here."

"Not nearly as grateful as we are to you," Madame Colette said. I looked at her curiously. It seemed so strange that someone like Madame Colette could be grateful to *us* for anything—but that was just the sort of person she was, always considerate, always kind.

"Now, I'm sure you are wondering about your new lodgings," Madame Colette continued. "I still need to give the matter some thought before I make a final decision, but you must trust me when I tell you not to worry. Henri and I shall always look out for you."

"We will be fine wherever you see fit to move us, madame," Mama said. "Camille and I will pack our belongings today."

"You will have as much assistance as you require from the staff," Madame Colette promised her. "I'll make an announcement at lunch. Thank you again for your flexibility. I knew I could count on you both."

Mama and I curtsied to her before we left the parlor. As soon as we were safely in the hall, I reached for her arm. "Oh, Mama—" I began.

She quickly shook her head, and I knew that she wanted me to be quiet until we returned to the kitchen. But what I had to say couldn't wait.

"Can't I tell her about your ankle?" I said in a whisper. "Please, Mama, all those stairs—"

"No, Camille. We will not make a bother of ourselves to the Rousseaus," she replied in a hushed voice. "Madame Colette has told us not to worry; she has promised us that she will take care of us, and so we must follow her orders the same way we would if she asked us to make a crème brûlée or a tray of petits fours."

I bowed my head. Mama was right, of course, and I was ashamed that I hadn't realized that sooner.

"Chin up, my little butterfly," Mama said as she wrapped her arm around my shoulders. "All shall be well."

I wanted to believe her; truly, I did.

But that was easier said than done.

When it was time for the noonday meal, I took my place at the crowded table in the servants' common room without any appetite. There was a tureen of creamy carrot soup and a loaf of crusty bread for us to share, but I didn't think I could swallow a single bite. With so many guests staying in the servants' quarters, we ate supper in shifts to make sure there was room for everyone at the table, but the midday meal was an exception in which all the servants ate together.

As promised, Madame Colette soon appeared in the doorway. We all stood up at once.

"Please, please, be seated," she said warmly. "I'm sorry to interrupt your meal, but I have an important announcement to make. Tomorrow we will be joined by a new family, who have endured months of hardship since the flood. They are Bernadette's relations, and I know that we will all do our best to see that they feel welcome here."

I looked over at Bernadette, along with the rest of the servants. She seemed positively gleeful to hear the news announced officially. The servants knew better than to grumble in front of Madame Colette and Bernadette, but I saw worried glances pass among several of them.

"Happily, I expect that this addition will help to lessen your workload—not increase it," continued Madame Colette. "Bernadette's cousin and his son will be taking on all groundskeeper responsibilities, while I am told that the wife is a fine cook who will be glad to oversee the preparation of meals for you and your families, freeing the kitchen staff so that they may return to their usual tasks."

Now all eyes turned toward Mama and me. I'm sure they were all wondering the same thing: If a new groundskeeper had been hired, where would we go?

"Marie and Camille have graciously agreed to vacate the groundskeeper's cottage first thing tomorrow morning to make room for our new arrivals," Madame Colette said. "I trust that you will give them every assistance they require. To that end, Jacques and Maurice, I would ask you to move their personal belongs to the three unused rooms on the second floor of the West Wing. Josephine and Renée, please see that those rooms are aired out today. They shouldn't need more than a light dusting to make them suitable."

*The second floor?* I thought. *Of the West Wing?*

Surely I had misheard her.

Madame Colette hadn't just announced that Mama and I would be moved to the second floor of Rousseau Manor.

Had she?

Such a thing would be impossible!

*To live in Rousseau Manor!* I thought, overcome with glee. *On the second floor, no less!* Why, the Rousseaus themselves had their private chambers on the second floor of the East Wing! It would feel like we were family!

Of course, that was a silly thought, and I immediately pushed it out of my mind. I was just a servant—just a servant's daughter, really—and it was important for me to remember my place. But when I glanced around the table, I saw that Mama looked as amazed—and as astonished—as I felt. Just as quickly, though, Mama composed herself, sitting beside me as calm and collected as if Madame Colette had merely remarked on the weather. I quickly tried to follow her example. There would be plenty of time later to celebrate when I wrote all about it in my journal, when no one was watching.

At that moment, I had the most peculiar feeling that someone was watching me. I rubbed the back of my neck, which had gone all prickly and cold. My gaze traveled the length of the table until I saw her:

Bernadette, staring directly at Mama and me, with a look of absolute loathing on her face. Our eyes met for the briefest instant—just long enough for me to see how dark hers had grown. A heavy feeling of unease settled over me.

*Oh, no,* I thought. *What have I done now?*

3

$\mathcal{J}$acques and Maurice arrived at our cottage before dawn the next morning so that they could move us into Rousseau Manor without disrupting Monsieur Henri and Madame Colette. Mama and I were dressed and ready, with our belongings packed into three small boxes and a carpetbag. Almost everything would stay in the cottage—the comfortable armchair where I loved to curl up with a book on rainy Sunday afternoons, the washstand with its porcelain bowl and pitcher, the heavy oaken table where Mama and I had shared so many breakfasts. All the other servants dined together in the common room, but since we were lucky enough to have our own kitchen in the cottage, Mama and I always rose early enough so that we could eat breakfast together in the mornings. Our meals were plain, of course—boiled eggs or porridge—but those quiet moments with Mama, just the two of us, were something I would always treasure. Especially, I realized with a pang, since they were now a thing of the past. Without a kitchen in our new rooms, Mama and I would be eating all our meals with everyone else.

*Shame*, I thought to myself sternly. *It is a privilege to move into Rousseau Manor. It is a privilege to be given three meals a day.*

"Ready to go, Marie?" asked Maurice as he lifted the largest box.

"Yes, Maurice. Thank you so much," Mama replied. "Camille and I are so grateful for your help!"

"I suppose these two boxes belong to you, Miss Fancy," Jacques teased me as he lifted the smaller boxes, one on top of the other. My face started to grow hot. Jacques was the youngest footman. He'd been at Rousseau Manor for only six months. Most of the staff thought that he was friendly and fun; he was certainly the most popular of all the servants. But Jacques had a knack for teasing that always embarrassed me, as though he knew just what I was most sensitive about— or what was most likely to catch Mama's attention. And sure enough, I caught a warning glance from her.

"Oh, Jacques, you mustn't tease the poor girl," she

chided him. "Everyone can see that there's nothing fancy about Camille."

Jacques's grin was full of mischief. "No, not in her dress, I suppose," he agreed. "But by the way she talks, she belongs in the West Wing. Or at least she thinks she does!"

"That's enough, now," Maurice told him, but it was too late for me; I was already blushing miserably. Monsieur Henri and Madame Colette had shown me so much favor over the years that I really did speak more like them than the other servants—especially since they had arranged for a private tutor to come to the house twice a week to instruct me in writing, grammar, arithmetic, and manners. When my lessons began, Mama had warned me about this very thing. She had said that if I wasn't careful, people might think I was putting on airs. Remembering to speak one way for the Rousseaus and my tutor and another way for my fellow servants was a challenge, even after years of practice. But it was clear from what Maurice was saying that I had to try harder. It simply wasn't right for me to give off the impression that I think I am above any of the other servants. I know I'm not.

I snapped out of my thoughts when I saw Mama lifting the carpetbag. "No, Mama. Let me carry it!" I exclaimed. Dr. Olivier had told her not to tax herself since her fall, but she was determined to do everything just as she had before.

"All right, Camille," Mama said. Then she leaned close to my head and whispered, "Pay no mind to Jacques's little jokes."

I smiled at her in response as we followed Maurice and Jacques into the dawn. I paused, just briefly, to look over my shoulder one last time at the little cottage. It had been home for so long, but by tomorrow a new family would be living there. *I hope they love it as much as Mama and I did,* I thought.

Then I turned around to face Rousseau Manor—and our future! Ever since Madame Colette's announcement, I had longed to sneak into the West Wing to see our new rooms for myself. But I knew better than to do that, especially with the housemaids preparing them. I would hate for anyone to think that I was gloating about our wonderful new situation. So instead I had busied myself in the cottage, daydreaming about what our new rooms might be like while I packed all our belongings so that Mama could finish making the croquembouche.

There was already a tremendous bustle downstairs at Rousseau Manor; the kitchen staff was hard at work preparing breakfast while the housemaids began their daily tasks. But upstairs, Madame Colette and Monsieur Henri were still in bed; it was as silent as a tomb. We slipped up the servants' staircase as quietly as we could, not wanting to disrupt their rest. The whole way, I tried to temper my expectations. These were spare rooms, little used and never needed. They were sure to be simple and plain.

But my imagination could never have prepared me for what I saw when Maurice opened the door.

"Do you need anything else?" Maurice whispered as he gently set our boxes in the entryway.

"No. Thank you very much," Mama said.

"See you downstairs, then," he replied.

Jacques gave me a sly smile. "Enjoy your new lodgings, Miss Fancy," he said in a low voice. Then he disappeared behind Maurice, and Mama quietly closed the door behind him.

"Oh, Mama!" I exclaimed in delight the moment we were alone. "It's so—so—so—"

"I know," she said as she reached out and hugged me.

"It's so grand!" I cried as I ran from room to room. There were *three* rooms, just for us! We had our very own sitting room with a full set of comfortable furniture, and there was a large gray bedroom for Mama with a luxurious four-poster bed. And just beside it was a room for *me*. I knew it had to be mine, because there was a darling plush bear perched on the bed, as if he were trying to welcome me to my new room. Madame Colette was always spoiling me!

I rushed over to the bear and gave him a hug. His arms and legs were jointed so that it almost seemed as if he could hug me back! And his velvety fur felt so real and soft.

"Mama, can you believe it?" I marveled. "My very own bear! It's too much. All of it is *too* much!"

When she didn't answer, I ventured into the gray room, where I saw Mama trying on a smart new hat. So Madame Colette had left a welcoming present for her, too!

"What a beautiful hat," I said. "Oh, Mama, you look so elegant!"

Mama smiled at me in the mirror. "We are very

could sit and rest when she finished in the kitchen would have to come first.

I decided to start in the gray room that belonged to Mama. Madame Colette had seen to it that Mama would have everything she needed in her new room: There was a comfortable bed and a nightstand, a dresser with a shiny mirror hanging over it, a coatrack, and a hat rack. I opened the carpetbag to unpack Mama's clothes. She didn't have much—a spare work dress, a Sunday dress, and a coat. Three extra aprons, two nightgowns, and her underclothes. I had them put away in no time.

On Mama's dresser, I carefully spread out the lace doily that Mama had tatted when she was a girl. Then I arranged the hairbrush that had belonged to her own mother alongside a packet of hairpins. Finally, I placed the photo of Mama and Papa from their wedding day. It was the only photo we had of Papa—which made it Mama's most treasured possession.

It had been seven long years since Papa had died of influenza, but I could still remember so much about him—the way he let me help him in the gardens even though Mama protested that the sun-drenched work would give me freckles (she was right). The way he carried me on his shoulders when my little legs grew too tired to walk. The way Mama and I laughed as we plucked grass clippings from his fine blond hair before we all sat down to supper. Mama's hair was even lighter than his, the color of wheat just as it begins to turn golden at the height of summer. In the photo, they looked so young and so much in love. How cruel that Papa had died just five years later.

I returned the photo to its special place and took a long look around Mama's room. Then, satisfied that it was ready for her, I went to my own room to unpack. It seemed dreadfully unfair that I should have so many more belongings than Mama, but the truth was that Madame Colette and Monsieur Henri spoiled me terribly. Monsieur Henri always remembered me when he traveled, returning with sweets and picture post- cards and scenes for my stereoscope. I even had a globe of the world that spun around with just a flick of my finger—and now my very own bear!

By the time I had finished arranging my room, though, it was nearly lunchtime. Even though I longed to write in my journal, it would simply have to wait—because there was nothing that could stand in my way when it came to Tuesday luncheons!

When I got to the kitchen, I saw that one of the scullery maids was putting the finishing touch on Monsieur Henri's tray—a delicate rosebud in a crystal vase.

"Where've you been all morning?" the head chef, Mrs. Plourde, called to me.

"I was—I was unpacking," I told her.

"Ah, of course," replied Mrs. Plourde. "And are the rooms to your liking?"

"Oh, yes," I began, but Mama interrupted me.

"They'll be fine," she said. "Of course, we'll take extra pains to avoid disturbing the family."

Mrs. Plourde nodded knowingly. "Can't say that I'd like to live right under their noses like that," she replied.

That's when I realized that Mama was trying to make sure no one would feel jealous of our new situation. *She's so clever*, I thought.

Mama arranged a dozen piping-hot madeleines in a basket lined with a crisp white cloth. Then she placed it by the edge of the tray. "Mind the cookies. They're fresh from the oven," she told me.

"Just how Monsieur Henri likes them," I replied. *As do I,* I thought, but I didn't say it—even though it was no secret to Mama that he always shared dessert with me.

"The tray looks ready," Mama said. "Run along, Camille. You mustn't keep Monsieur Henri waiting."

"Yes, Mama, thank you," I said as I carefully lifted the heavy tray. In addition to the basket of cookies, it had a bowl of steaming asparagus soup and a plate piled high with ham and fresh vegetables from the garden. I could tell already that Monsieur Henri would be pleased.

I don't remember quite how it began, but for years now Monsieur Henri had requested that I serve his midday meal in his office every Tuesday. Monsieur Henri always said that eating at his desk allowed him to keep working without a break, but I can't imagine that he was able to accomplish much, since we spent the entire hour chatting about everything but his work! Monsieur Henri was a wonderful listener; I can't imagine that the silly stories of a servant's daughter were that interesting to him, but somehow he made it seem like the rest of the world slipped away while we chatted together. It was easy to pretend, during our wonderful conversations, that Monsieur Henri was my grandfather—a silly daydream that I could never mention to Mama, or even write in my journal.

As I approached Monsieur Henri's office door, mindful of the heavy tray in my hands, I noticed that it was closed. That was unusual—Monsieur Henri always kept his door open when he was expecting his lunch. I frowned. How could I knock while I was holding the tray? It would never do to place Monsieur Henri's food on the floor!

While trying to figure out what to do, I realized that I could hear voices carrying through the closed door. It was Monsieur Henri and Madame Colette, and they must have been speaking very loudly for me to hear them so clearly. Later I realized that I should have turned around and left immediately. But in the moment, I was so stunned that I paused and—I'm ashamed to admit—listened.

"The girl's parents are dead—dead!" Madame Colette said shrilly, each word louder than the one before. "She is *our* responsibility now! Don't you understand?"

"Of course I do," Monsieur Henri replied. "But it is complicated—"

"On the contrary, it is very simple," Madame Colette interrupted him.

"Please lower your voice, my dear," Monsieur Henri said. The rest of his words were a mumble. Then Madame Colette responded, also in a mumble, but whatever she said must have upset him, because I heard him answer, quite clearly, "What about Camille?"

What about me? What *about* me? Had Monsieur Henri really said *my* name?

"You act as if there is only one solution, and that it's a simple one, but you have given no consideration to Camille, who will be most affected if—"

*Crash!*

The tray!

Somehow, in my shocked astonishment, the tray had slipped from my hands, crashing to the floor with a terrible clatter. The carefully prepared vegetables had scattered across the hall; the ham sat in a greasy pool on the carpet; even the warm madeleines had crumbled into the puddle of soup. And worst of all, I'd broken the plate!

There was an immediate silence from Monsieur Henri's office. All I knew in that moment was that I had to get help.

*Mama,* I thought. *Mama will know what to do.* I felt better the instant I realized that she was right down-stairs in the kitchen. Mama could help me fix *all* of this.

As quickly as I could, I scooped up the tray and the china—especially the broken shards—and ran toward the stairs. I'd need a housemaid to help me clean up all that food, and we'd have to prepare a new tray for Monsieur Henri—and of course I'd have to make my apologies for the broken china—

But beneath all the thoughts rushing through my mind, there was one sentence that kept repeating itself, over and over:

*What about Camille?*

I'd heard only snippets of Monsieur Henri and Madame Colette's conversation, but somehow I just knew that something momentous had happened—and strangely enough, it had something to do with me. What I had heard made no sense, though. Who was this mysterious orphaned girl—and oh, how my heart ached for her; how terrible to lose *both* her parents—and how could her situation affect me? I was nobody, not even a servant yet—just a servant's daughter, trying my best to help and not get in the way or make more work.

Unlike dropping a tray full of food right outside Monsieur Henri's office.

Oh, what if he and Madame Colette opened the door and saw the mess before I could get back to clean it?

The very thought pushed me faster until I was nearly running into the kitchen, where my luck got worse. Because it wasn't Mama I saw as soon as I reached the kitchen.

It was Bernadette.

She took one look at me—I'm sure I was a mess, all disheveled from running, with strands of hair flying out of my cap—and the untidy tray and seemed to know exactly what had happened.

"Disgraceful," Bernadette said in a voice so cold that it sent chills down my spine. "Almost twelve years old, and you can't carry a tray of food to the master of the house without destroying his property?"

I bowed my head as tears of shame sprang to my eyes. "I'm sorry," I said hoarsely. But I knew that Bernadette's lecture had only begun.

Then Mama whisked toward us as fast as her injured ankle would allow. "Oh, Camille, what have you done?" she asked sternly, taking me by the arm. "You'll answer to me for this." She caught Bernadette's eye and shook her head ominously. I saw the hint of a satisfied smile flicker across Bernadette's lips.

Mama took me into the pantry and closed the door behind us. The moment we were alone, tears spilled down my cheeks. "It was an accident!" I sobbed. "I'm sor—"

"Of course it was!" Mama said in a soothing voice, making me realize that her sternness in front of Bernadette was all for show. Mama dabbed at my cheeks with her handkerchief and kissed me quickly on the forehead. "You mustn't mind Bernadette. Everyone in service makes mistakes at some point or another. What broke? The plate?"

I nodded miserably as I explained what had happened.

"That's all right. You'll make your apologies and

they'll take the cost of replacing it out of my pay, and it will all be over and forgotten," Mama said. "Now, in the future, try to balance the tray in the crook of your left arm, steadying it with your left hand, while you knock with your right. See?" Mama demonstrated for me, smiling warmly. I tried to smile back, but my face felt all wobbly. She could tell right away that something was still troubling me.

"What is it, Camille?" Mama asked in concern.

"I was—I was outside Monsieur Henri's office," I began. "And I heard him talking to Madame Colette. It almost—it almost sounded like they were arguing."

A frown crossed Mama's face. "Camille, you know better," she said, and it hurt me to see the quick flash of disappointment in her eyes. "We must *never* listen at doors. *Never.*"

"I know!" I said right away. "It all happened so fast—you see, they were talking about a girl whose parents had died, and then I—I heard my name!"

"*Your* name?" Mama asked in surprise. "No, no, Camille, you must be mistaken. There would be no reason for Monsieur Henri and Madame Colette to mention you."

"But I—"

"No reason at all," she continued firmly.

"You're right, of course," I replied, already beginning to doubt myself. *But I* know *I heard my name*, I thought. *I'm sure of it.*

I looked up at Mama, searching her pale blue eyes. "Do you know what's happened?" I asked. "Who this poor orphaned girl might be?" Word traveled fast at Rousseau Manor, especially in the kitchen; sometimes the servants seemed to know more about what was happening than even the Rousseaus.

"No. I haven't heard a thing," she said, shaking her head. "But whatever's happening, we will be made aware when the time is right."

And as I looked into Mama's familiar eyes, I was certain she was right—just as certain as I was that I had heard Monsieur Henri say my name.

The next morning, Mama and I woke up extra early for some additional work in the kitchen. Bernadette's relatives, the Archambaults, were due after lunch, and we wanted to make sure that they felt welcome from the first moment they arrived at their new home. So we planned to surprise them with a basket of *pain au chocolat* as a welcoming present! While Mama prepared the special croissant dough, I carefully chopped up a block of bittersweet chocolate. Then she showed me how to make neat little parcels of dough with the chocolate tucked inside. The rich scent of butter and cocoa filled the whole kitchen while the *pain au chocolat* baked. When Mrs. Plourde told me to make some bread for the servants' lunch, I tried to remember Mama's directions exactly, since Bernadette was even more snappish than usual. That was very surprising to me, as I thought she would be happy to have her relatives joining her at Rousseau Manor.

Around midafternoon, the bell rang to summon Bernadette upstairs. "They must be here," she said distractedly, as she smoothed her apron skirt. "I'll be right back."

I felt a surge of excitement as Bernadette hurried out of the kitchen. I couldn't wait to meet the new family, especially the daughter I'd heard about. Perhaps she would join my lessons. We could have a little school! And most of all, I hoped that the new girl would be my friend. I'd never really known a girl my own age before; a friend of my very own seemed like a wonderful thing to have.

A few minutes later, Bernadette returned to the kitchen, with her relatives trailing behind her. She clapped her hands loudly to get everyone's attention. The servants immediately assembled into a line; I scurried across the room so that I could stand next to Mama.

"I'd like to present Philippe Archambault and his family—Élise, Alexandre, and Sophie," Bernadette announced. "As you know, Philippe will be the new groundskeeper, assisted by Alexandre. Élise will be joining all of you in the kitchen, preparing staff meals. I know that you will welcome them kindly."

Then Bernadette led her relatives down the line, introducing each member of the kitchen staff in turn. I craned my neck curiously, trying to get a better look at the newcomers while I stifled my disappointment. Little Sophie was only a baby cradled in her mother's arms; she couldn't have been even a year old! I loved looking after sweet little babies whenever the Rousseaus' guests arrived with children in tow, and Sophie was as cute as could be, but she was hardly the playmate I'd hoped for. I was also surprised to see the boy, Alexandre. I'd thought that Bernadette had told Madame Colette he was fully grown, but he couldn't have been much older than me. Neither one of the Archambault children were what I'd expected.

"And this is our pastry chef, Marie LeClerc, and her daughter, Camille," Bernadette sneered when she reached us. I smiled my brightest, but it lasted only a moment, because the faces looking back at me were cold as ice.

"Welcome to Rousseau Manor," Mama said as she held out the basket of warm *pain au chocolat*. "Camille and I made these for you. We thought you might be in need of some refreshments after your journey today."

Philippe and Élise exchanged a pointed glance, but I couldn't figure out what they meant by it.

"Thank you, but we won't take time to eat," Philippe replied. "We must get right to work."

"Surely not," Mama protested. "I know that Madame Colette would want you to settle in to your new home."

"No, thank you," Élise said shortly. "*We* don't need special treatment. We're here to work hard, not to be coddled and spoiled. I will be back shortly to prepare the servants' dinner."

A smug smile settled on Bernadette's face. "And that is why I spoke so highly of you to Madame Colette," she said. "Come now, I will show you to the cottage, and then you can begin your duties."

Philippe and Élise followed Bernadette without another glance in our direction, but Alexandre looked over his shoulder at us curiously, as though he were confused by something. The whole encounter left me feeling unsure and unsettled, especially when I realized that they had left the *pain au chocolat* behind.

"Wait!" I started to say, but Mama put her hand on my arm.

"It's all right, Camille," she said in a low voice. "But you can have one if you want."

Within the hour, Élise returned, wearing a clean apron over her cotton dress and carrying Baby Sophie in a wicker basket. "I am here," she said breathlessly, as though she had run all the way from the grounds-keeper's cottage. "I am ready to work."

Mrs. Plourde took a long look at Sophie. "With the child?" she asked bluntly.

"Sophie is very well behaved," Élise assured her. "You will soon forget she is even here."

"All right, then," Mrs. Plourde replied, but she didn't look convinced. "You'll find vegetables in the pantry; you probably have enough time to make soup. Camille is making the bread, so that should be ready by supper."

"Thank you, Mrs. Plourde," Élise replied.

I continued to knead the dough silently, watching out of the corner of my eye as Élise set the basket in the corner. She placed a simple rag doll in Sophie's hands and whispered something to her. Then Élise filled her apron with onions, carrots, and celery. She looked around the kitchen helplessly for a moment.

"The knives are over there," I told her, trying to be helpful. "In the drawer beside the stove."

Élise looked at me in surprise. "Thank you," she said coldly as she hurried off to get a knife. But by the time she had returned, Sophie had started climbing out of the basket!

"No, Sophie!" Élise said sternly. "You stay *in* the basket. Stay *here!*"

"Mama!" Sophie cried, holding her arms out.

Élise shook her head. "Mama is cooking," she told the baby. "Mama cannot hold you right now."

"May I hold her?" I asked.

"That won't be necessary," Élise told me. "Sophie always minds me." Then she crossed the kitchen and started a fire under the enormous stockpot.

I kept kneading the loaves of bread, watching Sophie out of the corner of my eye. While Élise melted butter in the pot and chopped the onions, Sophie was good as gold, hugging her doll. But all too soon, Sophie grew bored and began to climb out of the basket again. I glanced anxiously at Élise, who had her back to Sophie as she stirred the sautéing onions. It would be so easy for me to tend to Sophie . . . but Élise had already told me not to interfere.

Just as I began to call for Élise, Sophie managed to tip over her basket! With a triumphant giggle, the baby began to crawl across the room. "Élise!" I cried urgently as I rushed over to Sophie and scooped her into my arms. The busy kitchen, full of sharp objects and boiling pots, was no place for a baby to crawl around.

Élise dropped her spoon at once. "Naughty girl!" she scolded Sophie. "Naughty! Mama said to stay in your basket."

"I would be happy to—" I began.

"It's not your concern," Élise interrupted me.

I turned away, stung. Why did Élise dislike me so much? I was only trying to help!

Behind me, I could hear Élise whispering urgently to Sophie, begging her to stay in the basket. Suddenly, the bitter smell of burning onions filled the air. I wrinkled my nose.

"Who is burning the meal?" Mrs. Plourde barked.

Élise gasped and rushed back to the pot. She turned

down the heat right away, but it was too late; a smoky cloud hung over the stove.

"I need to start again," she told Mrs. Plourde.

But the cook shook her head. "No time for that," she said.

"I understand," Élise said. She tried to scrape the burned bits off the bottom of the pot, then added a pitcher full of water. "Oh!" she suddenly exclaimed. "I forgot the carrots and celery!" She tossed them into the pot in such a hurry that water splashed over the side.

I frowned a little. I'd seen Mrs. Plourde make soup hundreds of times; she always sautéed the onions, carrots, and celery together before adding water, herbs, beans, and lots of salt and pepper. *I'm sure Élise's way will taste just as good,* I told myself.

"Mama-mama-mama," Sophie began to chant. "Mama-mama-mama-mama-mama-mama-mama—"

"Sophie, *hush!*" Élise snapped.

Mama and I exchanged a glance. I could tell that we were both thinking the same thing: This was never going to work!

"You've got to help with the baby, Camille," Mama whispered to me.

"I tried!" I replied. "But Élise doesn't want me to hold her."

"Mama-mama-mama-mama," chanted Sophie.

"Élise?" Mama called across the kitchen. "Camille is wonderful with children, you know. She—"

"Mama-mama-mama-mama-mama—"

"—would be more than happy to—"

"Mama-mama-mama-mama-mama—"

"Sophie!" Élise yelled. "Be quiet!"

The kitchen was completely silent for a moment. Then, to my astonishment, Sophie threw the little doll at her mother.

*Oh, no!* I thought in horror as the rag doll arced through the kitchen. *It's going to land in the soup!*

But what happened was much, much worse; the doll bounced off the pot, grazed the fire, and burst into flames as it fell to the floor!

"Out of my way!" Mrs. Plourde bellowed as she charged across the kitchen. She stomped on the doll as hard as she could until the flames were extinguished, leaving a charred mess on the floor. I was sure that Sophie's wails could be heard throughout all of Rousseau Manor.

Then Mrs. Plourde turned to Élise. "The kitchen is no place for a baby," she said sternly, shaking her spoon. "You'll need to make other arrangements, or I'll ask Madame Colette to make them for you."

"Yes, Mrs. Plourde," Élise said meekly, her head bowed.

I tried to catch Mama's eye again, but she wouldn't look at me.

But from the expression on her face, I knew that Mama felt just as worried as I did.

That night, Mama and I had the evening free to tend to our laundry. It had been a dreadfully dull chore to toil away at the washer all by myself while Mama was laid up with her broken ankle, but I was glad to make sure that we always had clean, fresh clothes. I was both surprised and delighted when Mama felt strong enough to limp down to the basement and keep me company; she could make even the laundry fun!

She perched on a tall stool across from me and watched as I added the soap flakes to the water. "Not so much, not so much!" she scolded me with a grin. "You'll be rinsing for days!"

"I wouldn't need so much soap if *someone* were less sloppy with the butter," I scolded her right back, until we both dissolved into giggles.

All of a sudden, Mama's smile faded, and she held a finger to her lips. I listened carefully until I could hear it too: the sound of someone crying. Bernadette was strict with the staff; there was to be no crying at Rousseau Manor, no matter what happened. So the servants learned quickly to find a private hiding place to tuck themselves away if they ever needed to have a good cry. The basement, though, was the worst sort of place—it wasn't a bit private, not with the laundry and the larder and various storage rooms.

But someone new to Rousseau Manor might not know that.

Mama slipped off the stool, wincing slightly as her feet hit the ground. I followed her around the corner, and there we found Élise, leaning against the wall, her shoulders shaking with sobs.

Instantly, Mama wrapped her arms around her. "There, there," she said soothingly. "There, there. Whatever's wrong surely isn't worth this much upset."

Élise tried to speak, but just shook her head as the tears cascaded down her cheeks.

"What happened?" Mama asked, her voice full of kindness. "You can trust us, Élise. Whatever it is, Camille and I will do everything we can to make it right."

"I—I—" Élise gulped.

"Deep breath," Mama reminded her.

Élise inhaled and exhaled. When she spoke again, her voice was calmer. "Dinner was a disaster!" she said. "I am so humiliated!"

"Oh, gracious, no!" Mama disagreed. "My dear Élise, what do you think the servants usually eat? *Blanquette de veau? Soufflé au fromage?* No, no, a simple meal of soup and bread is all we require."

"It was inedible," Élise said stubbornly. "You're trying to make me feel better, but I know the truth. I heard the footmen—what are their names again? The tall one, he said that it was slop not fit to feed the pigs, but since he was just a footman he might as well choke it down."

I grimaced. That *did* sound like something Jacques would say. And it's true that the soup wasn't very tasty, what with the burned onions, undercooked carrots, and thin, watery broth. But it was nourishing, with all those vegetables, and that's what mattered most of all.

"I'm not suited for this kind of work—not at all!" Élise continued as another tear slipped down her cheek. "I've only ever cooked for my little family, not a staff of thirty! I don't know the first thing about cooking for so many people!"

My frown deepened. How could that be true? Hadn't Bernadette told Madame Colette that Élise used to work in a restaurant?

Surely Bernadette wouldn't have lied to Madame Colette?

"You mustn't look at it that way," Mama told Élise. "Why, really, we're just a large family, after all. And I promise you that we're all quite used to simple foods. Now, tomorrow you'll be able to get your start bright and early, and I'll make sure that the scullery maids assist you with chopping and tasks like that. We may be a large family, but that just means that we have more hands to help out."

A look of hope brightened Élise's face. "Really?" she asked. Then she shook her head. "No, I won't be able to learn fast enough. I know it. And with Sophie—"

Élise's face crumpled up like she was about to start crying again, so I spoke quickly. "Please, Élise, I'd be so happy to watch her for you," I said earnestly. "She's such a sweet baby, and I love babies!"

Mama put her arm around me. "If you give her a

chance, you'll find that Camille is kind and responsible to a fault," she promised Élise. "I would trust her with my life."

"And I'm a disaster in the kitchen," I pressed on. "Ask anyone! I'd be much more useful minding little Sophie."

Élise hesitated. "I—I—" Then she sighed heavily as her shoulders slumped. "What choice do I have?" she asked.

It was far from an enthusiastic endorsement, but it would have to do. "Thank you, Élise," I said. "I promise I'll take the very best care of her."

"Now," Mama said to Élise, using her best take-charge voice, "dry your eyes, wash your face, and go home. You've had quite an eventful day, and I think a good night's sleep is just what you need."

Élise's eyes darted toward the stairs. "I should go to the kitchen and start preparing for tomorrow—"

"No," Mama said firmly. "I can do that for you. *You* need your rest."

Élise stared at Mama, as if seeing her through new eyes. "Thank you, Marie," she finally said. "I am very grateful to you."

"Not at all," Mama said as we walked toward the stairs. "Whatever we can do to make you feel at home is our pleasure."

But as we went upstairs, I noticed that Mama was limping more than usual. *She needs to go to bed herself,* I thought. *If she doesn't rest her ankle, it will never heal properly.*

I waited until Élise was out of earshot, and then I said in a low voice, "Mama, please, you must rest. Let me prepare the kitchen for Élise."

"I'm fine, Camille," Mama said, but there were lines of pain etched on her face. "I'm always happy to have your company, though."

"Please, I know I can get everything ready," I pressed.

"*You're* wanted upstairs," a new voice said.

It was Bernadette, looking more sour than ever. "And neither of you needs to trouble yourself with my cousin's work. Élise is quite capable on her own."

"Of course she is," Mama said quickly. "We only wanted to help ease her transition to life at Rousseau Manor."

"That won't be necessary," Bernadette said sharply.

"If Élise doesn't see fit to prepare the kitchen tonight, we will respect her choice."

"But—" I began.

Bernadette whirled around to face me. "Do you intend to argue with me and keep Madame Colette waiting?" she snapped.

"I'm sorry," I replied.

"I'll see you upstairs when you're finished, Camille," Mama said to me. From the look in her eyes, I could tell what had gone unsaid: that she would go right to bed and rest. As a wave of relief washed over me, I said my good-byes to Bernadette and Mama and made my way toward Madame Colette's bedroom. It was always a treat to spend the last hour of my day with her; I treasured the nights when she was home, without a ball or a benefit or an opera to attend.

I knocked on Madame Colette's door and waited for her response.

"Come in."

I entered softly, curtsying as I stepped into the room. Madame Colette's bedroom was a beautiful place, decorated in shades of shimmering pearl and rose. She kept the lamps low, so that they bathed

"I think babies are great fun," I said. "I used to dream of having a brother or a sister. But since Papa died . . ."

I noticed that Madame Colette had stopped brushing my hair, so I bit my tongue to keep from saying more. When I was alone with her, it was easy to forget my place. *Be still!* I scolded myself. Why would Madame Colette care about the silly dreams of a servant girl?

"It occurs to me that we should still have the pram from when *you* were a baby," she said as she began to brush my hair again. "It must be in the basement somewhere. If you'd like, I can have one of the footmen find it for you. Then you could take Baby Sophie for walks outside. The grounds are so lovely in the springtime."

"Oh, Madame Colette, that would be wonderful!" I exclaimed. Then I remembered Mama's warning not to ask extra work of anyone on the staff. "But, please, don't trouble the footmen on my account. I'm sure I can manage it on my own."

Madame Colette gave me a long look. "You know, Camille, I do believe you can," she replied. "It's made of wicker and is very light. And you are very strong."

I smiled, pleased by the compliment, as Madame Colette brushed my hair a few more times. "There," she said. "Smooth and shiny."

That was what she always said when she finished brushing my hair, and I knew that it was my cue to leave. But as I rose, she said, "One moment, my dear."

Then Madame Colette reached out and dabbed a bit of her lotion along my temples and at the base of my neck. I breathed in deeply, smelling the beautiful fragrance of lilies.

"Sweet scents for sweet dreams," she said. "Good night, Camille."

"Good night, Madame Colette," I replied with a curtsy. "And thank you!"

When Élise arrived in the kitchen with Baby Sophie the next morning, I was ready for her. "Good morning!" I cried. "Look at what Madame Colette has made available to us!"

Élise's eyes grew wide. "No," she breathed. "This pram is too fine—"

"She specifically said I might take Baby Sophie for walks in it," I assured her. "Apparently, it was *my* pram when I was a baby!" I found that hard to believe, but Madame Colette was no liar. What a pity that I couldn't remember being nestled among the pram's elegant satin pillows, with shafts of sunlight peeking through the slats of the white wicker!

I reached for Baby Sophie, who came into my arms willingly. "Hello, Sophie," I cooed. "My name is Camille. Would you like to take a walk outside? We can search for birds' nests in the apple trees!"

When Sophie started clapping her hands eagerly, I knew she approved of the plan. I tucked her in carefully among the pillows, then covered her with a blanket so that she wouldn't take a chill.

"You'll be all right by yourself?" Élise asked anxiously. "If you need anything—"

"Oh, yes, we'll be quite all right," I assured her. "I've grown up here. I know my way around the grounds better than anyone. Don't worry. I'll take the very best care of Sophie. We'll be back for lunch!"

Then, with Sophie waving happily, I pushed the pram into the courtyard.

"Out of our way, chickens!" I sang out as we strolled toward the path, making Sophie giggle as the chickens scattered, clucking at us. Soon we turned left, leaving the courtyard to follow the path through the flower gardens. It was a beautiful day, clear and sunny, with a brisk breeze that ruffled Sophie's pale brown curls.

"The apple orchard is my favorite place, Sophie, and I'll tell you exactly why," I said. I wasn't sure how much she could understand, but Mama had told me that it was very good to talk to babies so that they might learn more words. "In the springtime, like now, all the trees are covered with flowers, and they have the most beautiful scent! And then when the petals start to fall, it's like large, soft snowflakes drifting all around. Then in fall, the apples ripen! You'll love them, Sophie. They're so sweet and delicious and—"

Suddenly, I stopped. A chill ran down my neck. *Just the breeze*, I thought, shivering as I wrapped my arms around myself. I leaned over to make sure that Sophie's blanket was keeping her warm.

No. It wasn't just the breeze. Because at that moment, I spotted a flash of blue on the other side of the hedge. It was too pale to be a bluebird, and it was too early for forget-me-nots. It had to be someone wearing a blue shirt.

I pushed Sophie forward. "I know you'll love the orchard as much as I do," I babbled.

The blue flash moved beside us.

I stopped abruptly.

So did the streak of blue.

*Someone's* following *me!* I thought wildly. *What should I do?*

If I went back to the kitchen, I'd disrupt Élise's work and disappoint Mama. But I couldn't keep walking toward the orchard as if nothing were wrong. So I pulled myself up to my full height and said, as firmly as I could, "I know you're there, on the other side of the hedge. Show yourself!"

Nothing happened. I waited . . . and waited. . . .

As the seconds passed, I began to feel more annoyed than anxious. Here I was, having a perfectly lovely day, when someone saw fit to follow me? That was unacceptable!

I mustered all my courage and leaned toward the hedge. I saw a pair of green eyes and a shock of light brown hair. I recognized that hair; it was the exact same color as Sophie's sweet curls. *Alexandre?* I thought in disbelief. *Why is* Alexandre *following me?*

"I said show yourself!" I repeated, louder this time. "Or you'll leave me no choice but to send for Monsieur Henri."

It was an idle threat—I had no intention of disturbing Monsieur Henri for something so trivial. But Alexandre didn't know that.

At last there was a rustle in the bushes, and Alexandre sheepishly stepped through them. I looked around to see if he had shears or clippers or any possible reason to be lurking about the bushes, but he was empty-handed. He wasn't even wearing work gloves.

"What are you doing?" I asked. "Were you—were you *following* me?"

Alexandre looked down as he kicked at the dirt. He didn't say anything.

"*Well?*" I demanded.

"Yes," he finally admitted.

"Why?"

There was a long pause before Alexandre spoke. Then he jerked his thumb toward Sophie. "I . . . I had to look out for Sophie. She's my sister. Don't take offense."

"But I'm looking out for Sophie," I said, confused. "Don't you trust me?"

When Alexandre didn't respond, I had my answer.
"Oh," was all I could say. Then I asked, "Why not?"

Alexandre looked miserable, but he eventually said,
"Well—it's just—we don't know you! We don't know
anybody here! And if it's true what they say—"

"If *what's* true?" I asked.

"Never mind," he mumbled.

I stood there awkwardly, wondering how Mama
would advise me. Élise had been just as cold until
Mama reached out to her in friendship. Maybe that
would work with Alexandre, too.

"You don't know us *yet*," I said. "But all the staff is ready
to welcome you! We're all glad you're here. Everyone tries
to help, in any way they can—no matter what's asked of
them. That's how it's always been. I'm so glad to be useful
to your mother so that she can concentrate on her work
in the kitchen. You needn't worry about Sophie. I promise
you I'll take the very best care of her!"

Alexandre gave me a long look. It seemed awfully
silly, but I was suddenly struck by how, well, *handsome*
he was, with that shiny hair and eyes that were as green
and sparkling as Madame Colette's emerald necklace. I
looked away quickly.

"Come," I said, hoping that he didn't notice the red blush creeping into my cheeks. "Let me take you on a tour of the grounds. I'm sure that there's much for you to see. Unless your father needs you?"

Alexandre shook his head. "He's doing inventory in the toolshed today," he replied. "He told me to stay away on account of all the sharp, rusted pieces."

"I imagine it's in a terrible state," I said. "I'm not sure anyone's maintained the tools properly since my father died."

He gave me a quizzical look. "Your father?"

"Oh, yes. Papa was the last groundskeeper at Rousseau Manor," I told him. "He died when I was four, though, and since then all the landscaping has been done by day laborers."

"I'm sorry about your father," Alexandre said in a quiet voice.

"Thank you," I replied. Then I smiled. "I think he'd be happy that you and your father are here to put things right. Papa loved the grounds at Rousseau Manor. He tended them with joy and care."

For the next hour, I showed Alexandre all my favorite spots: the lily pond, the elegant marble fountain, and, of course, the apple orchard.

"It's a splendid piece of land; there's no doubt about that," Alexandre said. "But I'd hoped you might tell me about all those overgrown, brambly hedges behind the house. Papa can't wait to rip them out. Such an eyesore!"

"They weren't always," I replied. "They used to be a topiary garden—you know, bushes sculpted into a particular form. Papa trained the bushes to grow into the most fantastical creatures, a whole menagerie of them! There were monkeys, a lion, a pair of swans . . . even a peacock, with morning glories twined through the branches to look like feathers. But with no one to tend them over the years, they fell into disarray. Now you can hardly tell what each one used to be."

"Oh," Alexandre said, sounding surprised.

"It used to be my favorite place on the grounds," I confessed. "But not since they've become so overgrown. Now it just makes me sad to see them and remember how much Papa used to care for them. I wish you didn't have to uproot them all, though. But I suppose it's for the best if they've become a blight on the landscape."

Alexandre stared at the sky. "It must be almost time for lunch," he said abruptly, noticing the position of the sun.

"We'll go back, then," I said, turning Sophie's pram around. "I'm sure your mother will be glad to see that no harm's come to her baby."

When we arrived back at Rousseau Manor, though, the kitchen was empty. My forehead wrinkled in confusion. "That's odd," I said. "Usually the kitchen is bustling from morning until night."

There was only one thing that could account for the unexpected quietness. I scooped Sophie out of the pram as fast as I could. "Come on, Alexandre," I said. "Hurry!"

"Why? What's wrong?" he said urgently. "Where are we going?"

"Upstairs—to the salon!" I replied. "If no one's downstairs, it means that Monsieur Henri and Madame Colette have called an important meeting!"

Alexandre and I raced up the back stairs and down the hall to the salon, which was crowded with all the servants. They were chatting quietly among themselves, which was a good sign; if Monsieur Henri or Madame Colette had been present, the servants would have been silent, giving them their full attention. No doubt the rest of the servants were as curious about this mysterious meeting as I was!

As we slipped into the crowded room, Alexandre gestured to the last empty chair. "Please, sit," he said.

"Thank you," I replied. I dandled Baby Sophie on my knee, making her squeal with laughter as I jiggled her up and down.

Across the room, I spotted Élise smiling at us. She gestured as if to take Sophie from me, but I shook my head. "She's doing fine," I called, hoping that Élise could hear me over all the chatter.

Then Alexandre leaned down to tickle Sophie's

plump cheeks, making her giggle all the harder. The baby's laughter was infectious, and soon the whole room was chuckling . . . except for Bernadette, who stared at us with a hard look in her eyes. A sudden wave of self-consciousness made my smile fade. Was my apron mussed from my morning outdoors? Had my hair come loose from its orderly plait?

If I hadn't done anything wrong, why did Bernadette dislike me so?

Before I could ponder the question further, Madame Colette entered the room on Monsieur Henri's arm. The entire crowd quieted at once, except for Baby Sophie—but I knew her sweet babbling wouldn't bother our kind employers.

"Thank you all for gathering here on such short notice," Madame Colette began. "We know how hard you work and how busy you are. Please know that your efforts do not go unnoticed, and we are deeply grateful for them."

"Especially now, when Rousseau Manor is filled to capacity," added Monsieur Henri. "A lesser staff would have succumbed to petty quarrels and squabbling from the strain, but not you."

They paused for a moment to let their praise wash over us. I could tell that everyone was relieved. The Rousseaus were not given to public scoldings—in fact, such a thing had never happened at Rousseau Manor in my memory—but it was always a worry for servants that our employers would find fault with our work.

"We have an announcement that will undoubtedly take you by surprise," Monsieur Henri said. I noticed that his arm tightened around Madame Colette's waist; she grasped his arm so that they were supporting each other.

"It grieves me to tell you that my cousin Nicolas and his wife, Annabelle, were killed in an automobile accident in America," continued Monsieur Henri.

Such tragic news! The servants were too well trained to display much emotion, but I could see a stricken expression on nearly everyone's face. My heart clenched like a fist.

But the news only got worse.

"They leave behind a daughter, Claire, who is but eleven years old," finished Madame Colette. She closed her eyes, overcome.

*Eleven years old!* I thought as tears pricked at my

eyes. Poor, poor Mademoiselle Claire. When Papa died, I learned firsthand how heartbreaking it was to lose a parent. But to lose *both* mother and father. To be an orphan, alone in the world . . .

"We have, of course, extended our deepest sympathies to Claire and offered her a home with us here at Rousseau Manor," Monsieur Henri said. "And so I announce with great relief that her American guardian has accepted our offer on Claire's behalf. She will arrive in two weeks' time, and we will raise her as our own."

A low murmur surged through the room. My thoughts were all jumbled: I felt so sorry for Mademoiselle Claire, and yet I could hardly believe that a girl my own age would be coming to Rousseau Manor! I already knew that I would gladly do all that I could to ease her pain and make her feel at home here.

Before the servants could continue their hushed conversation, Bernadette rose from her seat; the mere sight of her towering over the crowd silenced everyone.

"If I may, on behalf of all the staff here at Rousseau Manor, I would like to offer my deepest condolences for your loss," she said in a solemn voice. "I give you my assurances that we will tend to Mademoiselle Claire with the greatest of care. It will be an honor to serve her, as it is an honor to serve you."

The strain on Madame Colette's face melted away as she placed her hand over her heart. "Thank you, Bernadette," she said. "My thanks to *all* of you. We are grateful to have you by our side in times of trouble."

"Madame, you are the one who has supported us in our time of need," Bernadette replied, gesturing to Philippe and Élise. All the servants who had relatives staying at Rousseau Manor nodded in agreement. "We are forever in your debt."

"Nonsense," Madame Colette said firmly. "We are glad to be of assistance. We won't keep you any longer today, but as I'm sure you all know, there will be a great many arrangements to be made before Claire arrives. So we shall continue this conversation in due time."

The servants rose as Monsieur Henri and Madame Colette left the room; as soon as they were gone, there was an eruption of chatter. Élise pushed her way through the crowd to Alexandre and me.

"Thank you, Camille," Élise said fervently as she

reached for her baby. "You really do have a way with children. Look how happy my little Sophie is to be with you!"

"She's darling," I told Élise. "It was my pleasure to watch her."

"It must be time for lunch," Alexandre said. "Let's go to the servants' dining room."

"Actually . . . you go ahead. There's something I need to do first," I said. I knew I should eat, but my appetite was gone. The only thing I could think about was escaping to my room for a few quiet moments to write in my journal. My feelings were too intense to keep bottled up inside me; I simply had to let them out, and writing was the best way.

"Oh, I see," Alexandre replied. Was it my imagination, or did he look a little disappointed? I smiled warmly at him and waved as I ducked out of the room.

As quickly as I could, I darted through the halls to my new room in the West Wing. Once inside, I went directly to the writing desk and sat down with my journal, my pen, and a fresh bottle of ink.

I am trembling as I write this, stunned by the news that Madame Colette and Monsieur Henri have just delivered to us. To think that Mademoiselle Claire will be coming to Rousseau Manor to live here! For so long, I have wished and hoped for a playmate—for a friend—my age. And yet it seems especially cruel that my wish comes true because of the tragic accident that has claimed the lives of Mademoiselle Claire's parents. My heart breaks for her, again and again and again, when I think of the pain she must be enduring. I wonder what Mademoiselle Claire thinks of coming to France. Is she frightened? Upset? Grateful for extended family who will take her in?

Does she even speak French?

It is safe to assume that the days and weeks ahead will be especially grueling for Mademoiselle Claire. I shall make it my sole purpose to offer her comfort in any way that I can. I understand—at least a little—how much her heart must be hurting right now. It has been seven years since Papa died, and I am starting to think that the pain of losing him will never fully go away.

I wish there were a way I could send Mademoiselle Claire some reassurance, to ease any fears she may have. From the excessive kindness that Monsieur Henri and Madame Colette have shown me, I know that they will shower her with love, just as if they were her grandparents. Just the way I wish they were mine.

"Camille."

Mama's voice wafted to me from the doorway. I looked up guiltily as I covered my writing with my hand. We both knew that I wasn't supposed to steal away during the day for something so trivial as writing in my journal.

"You were missed at lunch."

The gentle rebuke filled me with shame. How many times had Mama told me that it was especially important for me to follow all the rules? To make sure that no one could accuse me of putting on airs? Of taking advantage of the special favors from Madame Colette and Monsieur Henri?

"I'm sorry, Mama." I apologized right away. "I just—I just *had* to write a little—"

She smiled understandingly. "Such unexpected news does make life topsy-turvy," she replied.

"I can hardly believe it," I confided. "My heart aches for Mademoiselle Claire, and yet I'm excited at the same time. I can't wait to meet her, Mama! I'm sure we'll be the very best of friends!"

Mama's smile was replaced by a troubled expression. "Dear one, you must remember that Mademoiselle Claire is part of the Rousseau family," she said. "You are a servant. You two may be friendly, but you will never be friends—and certainly not best friends."

"I—"

"You will have very little in common with her," Mama continued. "Mademoiselle Claire is an

American; undoubtedly, she has been raised in a wealthy home, with all the luxuries she could ever desire. You are a servant, like me. We *serve* people like Mademoiselle Claire. We lead different lives from them; we have different fates."

"That's exactly my plan, Mama!" I exclaimed. "To serve her—to make her life here comfortable and familiar. That's just what I've been writing about!"

"Very good," she said, but her eyes still looked worried. "Now you must run along and eat something before all the food is gone. Then I'll require your help in the kitchen. I thought we'd make a strawberry galette for dessert tonight."

I smiled at Mama. Monsieur Henri loved strawberries, and the first crop of the season always brought him joy. I could tell that Mama had chosen the dessert just to please him in this time of sorrow.

"Put away your writing instruments and come to the kitchen. I'll set aside a bowl of soup for you," Mama told me before she left.

I blew on the ink to make sure it was dry, then carefully tightened the cap on the ink bottle to make sure it was completely closed. An ink stain in my fine new bedroom would be a catastrophe!

Then, all of a sudden, a genius idea struck me. *A fine new bedroom!* I thought in excitement. *That's just what I can do for Mademoiselle Claire!*

It would be perfect: There was a suite of empty rooms on the other side of the second floor. I couldn't imagine why they sat unused, year after year; to my mind they were the prettiest rooms in the house, with pink rosebuds on the wallpaper and sheer white curtains that let in the sunlight. It already had a tall wardrobe that would be perfect for Mademoiselle Claire's lovely gowns and an elegant four-poster bed with pink velvet drapes. I could clean it from top to bottom ... open the windows to air it out with the sweet spring breezes ... polish all the fine wooden furnishings ... and arrange everything in it *just so* for Mademoiselle Claire. That way, from her very first night at Rousseau Manor, she would feel at home.

I just needed to get Madame Colette's permission first.

I bit my lip as I glanced at the clock on the mantel. Mama had told me to go directly to the kitchen. Would she be upset if I made a stop along the way?

*I won't take but a minute of Madame Colette's time,* I told myself as I set off down the hall. Perhaps Mama wouldn't even notice that I was a tiny bit later than she expected. And that might have been the case if I hadn't run into Bernadette. Her eyes narrowed when she spotted me.

"What are you doing out of the kitchen?" she asked bluntly.

"There was something I needed to do in my room," I tried to explain.

She looked like she didn't believe me. "A note-worthy morning, wasn't it?" Bernadette asked, her eyes never leaving my face. "It's not every day when Rousseau Manor is rocked by such an announcement. That poor girl."

"Yes," I said, nodding my head. It was always safest to agree with Bernadette, and this time I truly did.

"And poor you."

For a moment I thought I'd misheard her. Poor *me?* That couldn't be right. "What do you mean?" I asked carefully.

"It's a sad day for you, that's all," Bernadette con-tinued. Her lips twitched as if she were holding back a laugh. "You must know that you won't be the Rousseaus' favorite anymore, not once Mademoiselle Claire arrives. They'll turn all their attention to her, their own blood relation, which I daresay is more appropriate—don't you agree?"

"Yes," I said numbly.

This time, Bernadette couldn't hide her smile any longer. "Well, try not to cry too much about it," she said in a voice that might have sounded friendly, if her cruel words didn't betray her true meaning. "It's not really *your* fault. I'm not one to speak ill of my employers, but everyone could see that this peculiar . . . situation would only end badly. Hurry along to the kitchen, Camille. Heaven knows there's work to be done."

I nodded my head, staring at the floor as Bernadette brushed past me. But as soon as she was gone, I continued on my way to Madame Colette's parlor, trying to shrug off Bernadette's hurtful words. *Of course* I knew that Claire was part of the Rousseau family and I was not. *Of course* she would hold an important place in Madame Colette's and Monsieur Henri's hearts— a place that I could never dream of having. But that didn't mean that all the special times I had shared with the Rousseaus over the year were meaningless. I would always be grateful for their attention—and what better way to show that gratitude than to do everything I could for Mademoiselle Claire?

I tapped quietly on the parlor door.

"Come in," Madame Colette called.

I slipped inside and curtsied, waiting for her to address me. She looked up from a stack of papers on her desk with a harried expression. "My dear Camille. What can I do for you?"

"Pardon the interruption, madame, but I was wondering if I might talk to you about Mademoiselle Claire."

Madame Colette nodded, so I pushed ahead.

"Have you chosen her rooms yet?"

Madame Colette blinked as if she couldn't quite focus on what I was saying. She began to shuffle through some papers. "Her rooms? Oh, gracious, no, not yet. There are so many arrangements to be made that choosing Claire's rooms hadn't even occurred to me."

"I could do it, if you want," I said eagerly. "I could get everything ready for her—I would make it so special and take such pains, if only you'd let me."

"I don't see why not," Madame Colette said in a distracted sort of way.

Joy surged through me. "Oh, thank you, Madame Colette!" I cried happily. "I thought the two spare rooms in the East Wing would be perfect for her. They're so prettily decorated, and everything in them is so dainty and sweet. I just have a feeling that she would love to have them for her very own—don't you think so?"

Madame Colette didn't answer as she scribbled a note in her datebook. It wasn't like her to be so distracted; normally she gave her full attention to anyone who was speaking to her. *It must be her grief,* I realized. *How impossible for her to concentrate on such trivial things when the loss of Monsieur Henri's relations weighs so heavily on her heart.*

"Thank you, madame," I said with another curtsy. Then I quietly saw myself out.

But once I was in the hallway, I gave in to my excitement and skipped all the way to the kitchen.

I could already tell that everything was going to work out perfectly!

$\mathcal{I}$ was busy from dawn until dark for the next several days, tending Sophie in the morning, assisting Mama in the afternoons, and preparing Mademoiselle Claire's room every spare moment in between! All the hours I'd spent helping the housemaids came to good use: I washed the bedclothes, dragged the rugs outside to beat the dust from them, and scrubbed the windows until they sparkled. Every muscle in my body ached by the time I finally went to bed each night, but I always fell asleep with a smile on my face, imagining how pleased Mademoiselle Claire would be when she saw her new room.

At last, everything was clean to my satisfaction: There wasn't a speck of dust to be seen, and the entire room, from the drapes to the rugs, smelled fresh and clean. I stood back to admire the result of all my hard work, but a frown soon settled across my face. I couldn't shake the feeling that there was something missing from this room. Something important. Something that would truly make Mademoiselle Claire feel at home.

"That's it!" I cried suddenly as I realized what the room lacked. It was clean and bright—but utterly impersonal. There were no pictures, no trinkets, no books, no toys. It could be a room in any house, belonging to any person, from a baby girl to an elderly grandmother. Mademoiselle Claire's room wouldn't truly be ready until it was filled with items she might like.

*What could I give her?* I wondered, thinking about all my belongings. Mama's words suddenly came to mind; Mademoiselle Claire was the daughter of rich parents. Nothing I owned, not even the finest gifts from the Rousseaus, would be suitable for her.

*Perhaps I'll need to ask Madame Colette to buy her some fine things,* I mused. Of course, Madame Colette had probably already thought about that … but what if she hadn't? A troubled air had settled over her; she was more distracted than ever. I'd even heard the housemaids gossiping about how deeply affected she was by her grief. No, I decided, the last thing Madame Colette needed at a time like this was to be bothered by such trivial matters as toys and books.

*Mademoiselle Claire must be very sophisticated,* I thought. *She is an American, after all, from a highly regarded family. Perhaps I could find her some books in the library . . . some poetry perhaps—*

Then an idea struck me that was so perfect I almost laughed out loud in relief! When I'd gone down to the basement to fetch my old pram for Baby Sophie, I'd stumbled across a whole box of poetry volumes that had been neatly packed away. At the time, I'd wondered why they weren't in the library with all the other books that belonged to the Rousseaus, but I hadn't given it another thought since then. Now, though, I knew exactly where those books should be: in Mademoiselle Claire's room, awaiting her imminent arrival!

I set off for the basement at once, remembering to get a few candles and the packet of matches on my way. The storage area of the basement was separate from the laundry and the larder, which was why I'd never been there before my first visit last week. All along the back wall, not far from where I'd found the pram, were boxes that had been carefully stacked, one atop the other. There was a thick layer of dust on the top boxes, but after all the cleaning I'd been doing, I didn't mind a bit. I carefully lifted the lid of the first box and looked inside. Yes, there were the poetry volumes on top, along with several illustrated volumes of fairy tales. The books were beautiful, bound in rich leather with golden edges on every page. I knew at once that Mademoiselle Claire would adore them.

I glanced at the other boxes, wondering if I should look inside them, too. *The more nice things for Mademoiselle Claire, the better,* I decided as I peeked inside another box. This one was filled with the most magnificent assortment of dolls I'd ever seen! I counted twelve in all, dolls of all shapes and sizes: a beautiful porcelain baby doll whose eyes opened and closed; an elegant doll dressed in a delicate silk gown, with a cascade of golden curls spilling down her back; there was even a doll dressed for tea who came with her own tiny china tea set! Each one was more special than the last, and for a moment I imagined what it would be like to own something so beautiful. To sit at a low wooden table with the dolls set around me, perched on tiny little chairs, having a tea party complete with real petits fours and delicate cubes made of real sugar to gently plop into the teacups. I had outgrown imaginary play like that a few years ago, of course, but it was still fun to think about for a few moments. But then I reminded myself that it was exactly that kind of silly daydreaming that made it seem to the other servants like I put on airs. Feeling pleased that I had stopped myself from continuing down a foolish path, I hugged each doll and whispered to her about the new girl who would love and care for her.

*What other treasures will I find down here?* I wondered, full of anticipation. The next box contained everything a young lady would need for her dressing table: several small atomizer bottles of scent, a silver-plated mirror on a stand, and a matching hairbrush that was engraved with an elaborate wreath of forget-me-nots circling the letter *C. This must have belonged to Madame Colette when she was a girl,* I thought as I loosened my braid and ran the brush through my hair. The feeling of the bristles made me shiver all over, for reasons I couldn't figure out, so I quickly returned the brush to the box and fixed my hair. *For Mademoiselle Claire,* I reminded myself. I was sure that she would feel a special connection to all these items, knowing that they had belonged to Madame Colette long ago.

The last box was filled with the most wondrous assortment of toys, including a menagerie of wind-up mechanical circus animals that moved! I laughed excitedly as I watched the little monkey clash his cymbals while a proud peacock strutted in a circle. There was even a pair of swans who leaned their heads together as if to share a kiss! I knew that Papa, who had taken such pains to shape the animal topiaries outside, would have loved them as much as I did.

*Perhaps they will bring a smile to Mademoiselle Claire's face in the midst of all her grief,* I thought.

By that point I'd made quite a mess of the basement—there were dolls and toys and books scattered all about me—so I carefully repacked each box. Only as I picked up one of the volumes of poetry did I make a truly startling discovery:

There was another book hidden inside it.

It tumbled to the floor and landed near my feet. I stared at it for a moment in surprise. Unlike the fancy poetry books, this one had a plain, burgundy-colored cover without a title. The name "Claudia" was written on the first page in perfect, tiny handwriting. *It's not*

*Madame Colette's book, then,* I thought. *I wonder who Claudia was. A servant girl, perhaps. Someone just like me.*

I knew I shouldn't read it, but my curiosity soon got the better of me, so I flipped to the middle of the book. I saw right away that it was some sort of diary.

**15 May 1898**

*There is no one in the world who knows the secret I am about to commit to these pages—*

Instantly, I slammed the diary shut, knowing full well that I had no right to read it—though I was even more curious about the diary than before. *I'll show it to Madame Colette and ask for permission to read it,* I thought as I slipped it into my apron pocket. Then a new thought occurred to me. *I need to ask permission for all of this. I don't have the right to take these things upstairs—even if they are for Mademoiselle Claire.*

There was just one problem: The Rousseaus had left early that morning for a trip to the center of Paris. They wouldn't be back until the next day. And I couldn't bear to wait so long to finish arranging Mademoiselle Claire's room!

94

*Mama will know what to do,* I thought as I made my way up the stairs. I'd go straight to the kitchen and ask her advice.

But Bernadette blocked the stairs

"What were you doing back there?" she demanded. Though there was a harsh scowl on Bernadette's face, I couldn't help noticing the gleeful look in her eyes, like a cat who'd caught a mouse in a trap.

"I—I—"

"If you've been sneaking around where you don't belong, you'd best have a good explanation!"

I swallowed hard. "I—I was looking for things to put in Mademoiselle Claire's room," I stammered. "I found some old—dolls, and books, and toys. I—I wanted to ask Madame Colette if—"

To my surprise, Bernadette's scowl melted away. She looked almost happy. "Oh! That's a wonderful idea, Camille!"

"It is?" I asked in surprise. Bernadette had never paid me a compliment before, in all the years I'd known her.

"But you don't need to bother Madame Colette with something so unimportant," she continued. "After all, those are the family's belongings, and Mademoiselle

Claire is family. Go right ahead and take whatever you want for Mademoiselle Claire's room, and set it up however best you see fit. I'm sure your efforts will make Mademoiselle Claire so happy—*and* the Rousseaus as well!"

Bernadette's enthusiasm was contagious; soon I was smiling as broadly as she was. "Thank you, Bernadette!" I replied. "I'll take these boxes upstairs right now!"

"If you need help, I can send for Maurice," she offered.

"No, that's all right," I told her. "They're not heavy."

"This will be such a . . . surprise," Bernadette said. "Don't worry. I won't tell a soul about what you've planned."

I grinned at her as she stepped aside, making room for me to climb the stairs. Could it be possible that Bernadette was finally willing to give me a chance? *Alexandre didn't like me very well when we first met,* I remembered. *But after we spent the morning together, he seemed to change his mind.*

I could only hope that the same thing would happen with Bernadette.

A few days later, I knocked on the door to Madame Colette's parlor. It was finally time to unveil Mademoiselle Claire's new room to the household, and I could hardly wait to show everyone how I'd transformed it!

As luck would have it, I found Monsieur Henri in the parlor too. "I'm so sorry about the interruption," I began, "but Mademoiselle Claire's room is ready now, if you would like to see it."

A smile as warm as the sun filled Madame Colette's face. "Splendid!" she exclaimed as she rose from her desk.

"I take it this means we can *finally* see what our busy little bee has been buzzing about?" Monsieur Henri teased me.

I grinned at them both. "If it pleases you," I replied with a curtsy, remembering the manners Mama had taught me.

As the Rousseaus followed me down the hall toward Mademoiselle Claire's room, my hands were trembling so much that I had to clench them behind my back, but I don't think that either Monsieur Henri or Madame Colette noticed. I could hardly wait to see their reactions when they saw Mademoiselle Claire's special new room!

As we approached the end of the hallway, I saw a group of servants clustered around the door; Bernadette was there, and Josephine and Renée, and Mama, of course. Just seeing Mama made me feel more at ease.

"Wait," Madame Colette said suddenly.

I stopped and turned around. To my surprise, there was no trace of the smile on her face; it had been replaced by a pinched, worried expression.

"This is not—" she continued, but Monsieur Henri cut her off.

"It's just a room, Colette," he said tensely, and his voice was sharper than I'd ever heard it before.

It was very obvious that something was wrong, but I didn't know what. As I searched their faces for answers, Monsieur Henri nodded at me. "Go ahead, Camille," he said in a kinder voice. He slipped a supportive arm around Madame Colette's waist. "Show us what you have done."

I tried to return his smile as we continued down the hall. I had a whole speech that I'd planned to deliver before I showed them the room, but all of a sudden it seemed out of place. Instead, I decided to simply open the door and let the room speak for itself.

As everyone followed me into Mademoiselle Claire's room, I took one last look around the room that I'd so carefully cleaned and arranged. Soon Mademoiselle Claire would arrive at Rousseau Manor, and she would surely make the room her own, moving things, taking some away, adding others. That was as it should be, of course. But for now this beautiful room was arranged just the way I would've wanted it set up for *me*, and I didn't want to forget a single detail of what I'd done.

The sheer curtains fluttered in the breeze as patches of sunlight danced across the rose-colored carpet. All the slim volumes of poetry had been carefully dusted before I'd placed them in the bookcase. I'd taken pains to wash each doll's clothing before I brushed and styled their hair; they looked truly lovely arranged in the curio cabinet. I'd polished the silver hairbrush and mirror until they shone as brightly as the moon. I had even spritzed one of the glass atomizers about the room so that the very air smelled like a meadow filled with wildflowers. All that was missing was Mademoiselle Claire.

*Waiting,* I thought suddenly. *It feels like the whole room is waiting for a little girl to come home to it.*

Then I realized that no one had said anything. Not a single word.

I turned around to look at the others. What I saw, I would never forget.

Poor Madame Colette—she must've been taken ill; something must have been drastically wrong with her. All the color had drained from her face, leaving her ghostly pale. Her trembling lips were moving, as though she were trying to speak, yet no sound came out. At last I heard a wordless, anguished cry escape from her mouth. She hid her face in her hands as her shoulders shook with sobs.

"Madame!" I cried, taking a step toward her. But Monsieur Henri held up a hand to stop me. He, too, looked ashen, but there was a fire blazing in his eyes as he wrapped Madame Colette in his arms.

"Camille," he said, pointing at me. The way he said my name made it sound like a crime. "You had *no right—no right—*"

I couldn't breathe.

Monsieur Henri pressed his hand over his eyes; when he removed it, the fire in them was gone, replaced by a deep, lonesome sadness.

When he spoke again, he addressed Bernadette as though I wasn't even in the room. "You will have these things packed up with the greatest care and returned to storage," he said. "Then you will—"

*"Don't!"* Madame Colette sobbed. "Don't take it all away! Not again!"

There was a long, strained silence, during which Monsieur Henri's age had never been more clear. His face seemed to turn gray for a moment before he straightened himself and said to his wife, "Of course, my dear. Whatever you desire."

Then Monsieur Henri looked over at Bernadette. "Please make it known to the staff that I do not want this room to be disturbed ever again. *Ever.*"

"Yes, Monsieur," Bernadette replied.

For a long moment, no one spoke; the only noise in the room was the heartbreaking sound of Madame Colette crying. At last Monsieur Henri turned to face me.

"You are *never* to go into this room or down to the basement again," he ordered.

I nodded mutely as Monsieur Henri led Madame Colette from the room, whispering soothing words to her. Even as they retreated down the hall, Madame Colette's sobs echoed back to us. Tears filled my own eyes, making my vision blur. Even so, I could see the distress on Mama's face—distress that I had caused her. *How?* I wondered, numb. *How did I manage to hurt everyone I care about? I was only trying to help.*

It was the worst moment of my life.

"*C*ome," Mama said to me in a low voice. "Come."

With her arm around my shoulders, Mama whisked me past the gawking housemaids, past Bernadette, whose gloating grin I could see even through my tears. *How could anyone smile at a time like this?* I wondered. Even if Bernadette was happy to see my humiliation, didn't she have any compassion for the Rousseaus? When I thought about the way Monsieur Henri's hand had shaken when he'd pointed at me, or the way that Madame Colette had seemed to crumple, overcome by her grief—

And to think that it had been all my fault. . . .

Well, I didn't understand how *anyone* could take pleasure in that.

Mama hurried me down the hall as fast as her ankle would allow; in moments, we were safely hidden away behind the door to our rooms. Only then did I let my tears fall freely. Mama folded me into her arms and held me tightly as my tears soaked her apron.

"Shhh, shhh," she whispered. "There, there. You mustn't cry so, Camille."

But nothing Mama said could bring me comfort now.

Mama brought me over to the settee and handed me a fresh handkerchief. I buried my face in it as if it were a mask that I could hide behind for the rest of my life. The only thing more overwhelming than my confusion and embarrassment was my shame. Somehow, some way, I'd managed to hurt the Rousseaus terribly—and all when I was trying to be useful. How had my plan to make Mademoiselle Claire feel welcome backfired so badly? Just the thought made me sob harder.

"Camille." Mama's voice was still gentle but firmer than before. "You must calm yourself. You will do no one any good if you make yourself ill."

I tried to take a deep breath. To my surprise, the rush of air did help me feel calmer . . . at least a little.

"What did I do wrong, Mama?" I asked in a trembling voice. "I never meant to—"

"Of course you didn't," she replied. She bit her lip as

a troubled frown settled over her face. "As best as I can figure, those things must've belonged to Mademoiselle Claudia. And that, I think, must've been Mademoiselle Claudia's room."

"Who?" I said, puzzled.

Mama sighed. "I bear some of the blame," she said. "I suppose I should've told you this before, but the time never seemed quite right. And to be honest, we've all known for years now that Mademoiselle Claudia was not to be discussed in this house. . . ."

I sat up a little straighter. I could already tell that Mama was about to tell me something important.

"Perhaps you thought that the Rousseaus were a childless couple," Mama said. "In fact, they were not. They were blessed with a beautiful child, a daughter called Claudia, and I am told that she was the very light of their lives."

"They have a daughter?" I asked, stunned. How could it be possible that I had never heard about her before?

Mama nodded. "I never met her, but your papa told me the story one night shortly after we were married," she continued. "You see, as Mademoiselle Claudia approached a marriageable age, Monsieur Henri and Madame Colette began to make arrangements to find her a proper husband. But it was already too late—Mademoiselle Claudia had fallen in love with the son of a German count. Neither family was pleased about the news, and there was a terrible argument when Mademoiselle Claudia confessed her love to her parents. Monsieur Henri lost his temper, your papa said. He forbade Mademoiselle Claudia to ever see her sweetheart again."

"Then what happened?"

Mama looked down. "Mademoiselle Claudia left that very night," she said. "In the morning, there was a tremendous commotion—the house was searched from top to bottom, inquiries were made in the village, but it was too late. She was already gone."

"But—but—where did she go?"

"To Germany," Mama replied. "To be with her true love. Monsieur Henri was so angry that he forbade anyone to speak of Mademoiselle Claudia ever again. It was as though she were dead. All the portraits of her—all her belongings—all of it was packed up and hidden away in the basement."

Mama dropped her voice even lower. "Papa told me that Monsieur Henri wanted Mademoiselle Claudia's things *burned*," she whispered. "But Madame Colette refused. She was so firmly against the plan—she so deeply believed that Claudia would return to them, that they would be able to heal the rift that had torn their family apart—that Madame Colette insisted that her belongings be kept for her, just the way she had left them."

"But they weren't kept that way," I said in confusion. "They were all packed up in the basement, right where my old pram had been stored."

"I admit that I don't know much about it," Mama said. "This all happened before I came to Rousseau Manor. I suppose at some point, even Madame Colette knew that it was time to pack up Mademoiselle Claudia's rooms. But she could never bear to throw away her daughter's possessions."

"Mademoiselle Claudia never came home?" I asked. "She never saw her parents again?"

Mama paused. "In all the years I've been here, no," she said. "Mademoiselle Claudia has never visited."

"So where is she now?"

"Who can say?" Mama replied. "It is a sad tale, so

very sad. Our lives are too short to let such disagreements come between us."

I remembered then how upset the Rousseaus were with me. My mouth went dry as sawdust. Mama reached out and took my hand.

"Will they ever forgive me?" I whispered.

"Oh, dear one, I am sure that they will," Mama assured me. "It was just a mistake. You overstepped your bounds, that's all. Such a thing was certain to happen eventually, with the way they—"

"What?" I asked.

"It's just that—the separation between servants and family exists for a reason," Mama told me. "When those lines are blurred, it can lead to unfortunate situations like this one."

"How will I ever make it up to them?"

Mama looked thoughtful. "Here is what you will do," she advised me. "You will stay out of their way. Give them some time for their tempers to cool, so that their hurt and anger is not so fresh. Then you will go to them and apologize. I'll help you figure out what to say. And from then on, you will always remember your place at Rousseau Manor."

Mama leaned back and gave me a long look. "Yes, you are old enough for more responsibilities of a servant," she said. "Taking care of Baby Sophie is a very good start. After Mademoiselle Claire has settled in, I shall speak to Madame Colette. We will find a proper role for you. I know the kitchen work is not your favorite. . . . Perhaps you would be more suited to the tasks of a junior housemaid. And one day, you might even be a lady's maid!"

I tried to smile at Mama, but it wasn't easy. The last thing I wanted to do at the moment was consider my future as a maid. After all the lessons I'd had, surely the Rousseaus had intended for me to be something more . . . a governess, perhaps. . . .

No, I immediately scolded myself. *That's the kind of thinking that got you into this mess. You're not something more, you never have been and you never will be. You're the daughter of a pastry chef and a groundskeeper, and the most you can ever aspire to be is a lady's maid.*

My face burned with embarrassment as I thought about all the mistakes I'd made. Picking *that* room for Mademoiselle Claire . . . bringing up Mademoiselle

Claudia's old belongings from the basement . . . and most of all, thinking that I meant something to Madame Colette and Monsieur Henri. Thinking that I was like the granddaughter they'd always wished they had. Thinking that I belonged at Rousseau Manor. Thinking that this beautiful place was my home and that they were my family.

It wasn't just silly. It was foolish. And it was time to put an end to that nonsense, once and for all.

Mama glanced at the clock. "Are you feeling better, dear one?" she asked as she gave me a hug. "I need to start this evening's dessert—"

"Yes, thank you," I replied. "But, Mama, if you have a minute . . ."

She waited patiently for me to continue. I took a deep breath as I tried to figure out how to say what was on my mind.

"I think Bernadette *wanted* this to happen."

Mama looked troubled. "How can you say that?"

"When I found those things in the basement, I was going to ask you for permission to bring them to Mademoiselle Claire's room," I explained. "But Bernadette saw me first and asked what I was doing. I explained everything and she—she said it was a wonderful idea. And she told me to do it all in secret . . . so that I wouldn't ruin the surprise."

Mama's frown deepened, but she didn't say anything.

"She *must've* known, though!" I continued. "About Mademoiselle Claudia . . . about those things . . . about how much it would upset the Rousseaus!"

"And that's why it must have been a misunderstanding," replied Mama. "Bernadette knows about Mademoiselle Claudia. I'm sure of it. So if she had truly encouraged you to move all of Mademoiselle Claudia's things back to her old bedroom, why, that would have been deliberately hurtful to the Rousseaus! I can't imagine that anyone here would want that."

"No . . . ," I said slowly. "I don't think that Bernadette wanted to hurt the Rousseaus. But . . . I do think that she wanted to hurt me."

"Oh, Camille," Mama said with a disappointed sigh. "Bernadette may have a short temper and an unkind disposition, but she would never *try* to do something so cruel to you. You mustn't let your feelings get in the way of your judgment."

"Yes, Mama," I said. But secretly I still wondered Bernadette had seemed so happy when she'd told me to move everything into Mademoiselle Claudia's old rooms. My memory of our conversation was clear as day; I was sure that I hadn't misunderstood her.

"Wash your face, fix your hair, and change your apron," Mama said as she rose. "You'll find you feel much better after you've freshened up a bit. Then come to the kitchen—I think Mrs. Plourde won't mind if you have some bread and honey before you get to work."

I smiled at her. Mama remembered how much a little snack of bread and honey always made me feel better when I was sad.

"Thank you," I told her.

She kissed me on the cheek. "In a few days, all of this will be forgotten," she assured me.

I could only hope that she was right.

I began to comb my hair as soon as Mama left, but everything in my room reminded me of Mademoiselle Claudia's possessions. My reflection looked the same in my mirror as it had in hers. . . . My plain hairbrush was the same size as her fancy one. . . . Even my bear made me think of her wind-up circus animals. Soon my face burned with embarrassment all over again. It was going to take me much longer than a few days to forget what I'd done. I wasn't sure how I could ever escape from my humiliation when I was surrounded by reminders of it.

Distracted, I opened my drawer for some extra hairpins. But it wasn't hairpins I found there.

"Oh, no," I breathed.

Right there, in the center of my drawer, sat the journal I'd found in the basement. In all the work I'd done to get Mademoiselle Claire's room ready, I'd forgotten all about it.

Now what was I going to do with it?

I could never read it; that much was certain. Never, ever. I didn't even want to touch it—not after what I'd done and how terribly I'd upset the Rousseaus. I picked it up gingerly, as though the diary were something dangerous. I'd wondered if Claudia had been a servant—but now I knew exactly who Mademoiselle Claudia was.

Knowing that the diary had belonged to the mysterious missing Mademoiselle Claudia made me even more tempted to read it. What secrets were hidden

113

within that worn leather cover? But I'd already overstepped my bounds. I knew too well that I shouldn't
read the diary. I shouldn't even have it.

But what was I going to do with it?

Monsieur Henri had forbidden me to ever go down
to the basement again, so I didn't dare try to return it.
There were too many people—too many prying eyes—
who might tell him if I disobeyed. And if Bernadette
really did desire to get me into trouble, it would be an
easy thing for her to accomplish if she caught me in
the basement once more.

But if this diary were found in my room . . . well,
that would be equally disastrous. No, it wasn't safe to
keep it here. I needed to find a proper hiding place for
it . . . a place where no one would find it . . . where it
wouldn't be disturbed. . . .

"That's it!" I cried aloud when I finally figured out
a solution. I could hide the diary in Mademoiselle
Claire's—I mean Mademoiselle Claudia's—room. The
entire staff knew not to enter the room under any circumstances. It would be safe there, among her things,
where it belonged.

There was only one problem: Just like the basement,

Monsieur Henri had forbidden me to go back to that room.

I sat there in turmoil for another moment, trying to decide what to do. At last, with a heavy sigh, I slipped Mademoiselle Claudia's diary into my apron pocket. The best I could do was hurry—and hope that no one saw me.

I opened the door and peeked into the hallway. It was empty—but I knew that a housemaid, or even Bernadette, could appear at any moment. Most likely, Madame Colette had taken to her bed to rest, and Monsieur Henri would probably spend the remainder of his day alone in his study. But if Bernadette saw me even glance at the forbidden room, she wouldn't waste a moment telling them.

I crept down the hall with one hand pressed protectively over the diary. My heart was beating so hard in my chest that it seemed even louder than my footsteps! But in moments, I had reached the room. Quick as a wink, I slipped inside it, shutting the door behind me.

I crossed the room and tucked the diary under the mattress of the canopy bed. It didn't seem right to place it on the shelf as though it were an ordinary book, when it was clearly so much more special. Then, though I didn't dare linger, I took one last look around. The room was still so beautiful to me— and so special, knowing that everything in it had once belonged to the Rousseaus' long-lost daughter. Of course I understood why those dear little dolls and sweet volumes of poetry brought such heart- ache to Madame Colette and Monsieur Henri. But it seemed infinitely worse to hide them away in the damp, dark basement, where they would be untouched and unloved.

From the corner of my eye I noticed something rustling out the window. I moved close to take a bet- ter look . . . and spotted Alexandre and his father entering the topiary garden with their arms full of tools. Tears filled my eyes again as I realized that they were about to start pulling out the bushes that Papa had so lovingly tended while he was still alive.

*Why today?* I wondered, my heart heavy with sor- row. *Why today, of all days?*

$\mathcal{F}$or the next several days, I moved through Rousseau Manor like a ghost—quickly, quietly, unheard and unseen. I busied myself from morning to night with work, gladly volunteering for the most unpleasant tasks—polishing the silver until my eyes burned from the stench of the polish, filling the coal scuttles at each hearth before the sun was up, feeding the pigs with all the smelly kitchen scraps. I even would've done the laundry, but everyone knew that I was banned from the basement. No one had said that I should be punished for what I'd done, but it seemed to me that I had to make amends somehow. Besides, the worst of the work always fell to the junior housemaids. Since that would soon be my lot, it was only practical to start now.

To my surprise, almost everyone on the staff was excessively kind to me. I'd worried that they would share Bernadette's glee, but instead I think they felt sorry for me. Even Jacques stopped his teasing—for a few days, at least. And one evening I found a paper-wrapped piece of toffee by my plate at dinner. Mrs. Plourde would never admit to leaving it, but everyone knew how fond she was of sweets. I soon realized that Mama was right: The staff here *was* my family, far more than the Rousseaus could ever be. If only I had understood that sooner.

My walks with Baby Sophie were truly the best part of my day—especially when she started cooing my name whenever she saw me! When I was caring for Sophie, I could leave behind the drudgery of house-maid tasks as we visited all our favorite spots. The one place I wouldn't take her was the topiary garden. What was the point, now that the bushes were being torn out? And to be honest, I didn't want to face the vast empty space—though surely Philippe and Alexandre would plant something else there instead. Something beautiful that would bloom in its own time.

The night before the Rousseaus left to fetch Mademoiselle Claire, there came a surprising message. I was busy scouring the soot-blackened stove when Bernadette came before me, wearing a sour expression.

"You've been summoned," she said shortly. "Madame is in her chambers."

I glanced anxiously at Mama, who looked as surprised as I felt. We had both planned that I would make my apologies in a few weeks, after Mademoiselle Claire had arrived and life at Rousseau Manor had returned to normal. I was utterly unprepared to face either one of the Rousseaus tonight. Mama and I hadn't even had a chance to practice my apology!

"Camille is not presentable," Mama said, gesturing to my sooty face.

"Come *along*," Bernadette insisted, pointedly ignoring Mama. "Don't keep Madame Colette waiting."

As if in a dream, I rose from the table and began to follow Bernadette out of the kitchen. Mama hobbled across the kitchen and grabbed my arm. She quickly tucked a few loose strands of hair behind my ears and whispered, "Speak from your heart, and all will be well."

The familiar kindness of Mama's touch made me feel better at once. And I felt better still when Bernadette disappeared into her office, leaving me to walk to Madame Colette's room alone.

After I knocked on Madame Colette's door, I closed my eyes and made a silent wish that she would welcome me to her chambers, as she had so many times before.

"Come in."

Through the closed door, Madame Colette's voice sounded as sweet and friendly as always—but perhaps she didn't realize that it was me. I took a deep breath, mustered all my courage, and opened the door. With my head bowed, I dropped into a deep curtsy.

"Madame Colette, I beg your forgiveness," I said. "I have caused you great heartache, and I am deeply sorry for all that I've done."

"My dear Camille!" Madame Colette exclaimed in surprise. "Why are you apologizing to me? It is I who should apologize to you."

I shook my head. "It was wrong to bring personal belongings upstairs from the basement—" I tried to continue, but Madame Colette quickly interrupted me.

"I am afraid that Henri and I were so shocked to see our sweet Claudia's belongings in her old room that we completely lost control of our emotions," Madame

Colette spoke over me. "I hope you will be able to forgive our show of grief and temper."

"Oh, madame—" I began.

"You did a lovely job fixing the room for Mademoiselle Claire," Madame Colette told me. "Truly, no one could have done finer work than you. If it were not for the emotional attachment we have to those old things . . ."

Madame Colette shook her head. Then she smiled. "Come," she said, beckoning to me. "I feel as though I haven't brushed your hair in an age."

As I drew closer, though, her smile faded. "Camille! What is the meaning of this?" she asked in concern, reaching up to touch my sooty face.

"I beg your pardon," I said again. "I was cleaning the stove when Bernadette came for me—"

Madame Colette's frown deepened. "That's dirty, dangerous work," she said. "Who told you to do that?"

"No one did," I replied. "But, well, I know that Mama will approach you soon about this, but she thought it was time that I specialize. Either in the scullery, or perhaps as a junior housemaid. Whatever you think is best."

"No, no, no," Madame Colette said. "I won't hear of it. And you will not do such work again. Do you understand? Monsieur Henri and I have other plans for you, dear Camille."

My heart soared when she said that. *A governess—I knew it!* I thought. "What do you mean?" I asked eagerly.

"Now is not the time to discuss it, I'm afraid," she told me. "Come, let me help you."

Madame Colette dampened one of her fine muslin facecloths with the sweetly scented lavender water she always used. Then she cleaned all the soot from my face. I was ashamed at how black her facecloth grew, knowing she'd have to throw it away when she finished, but Madame Colette didn't seem to mind.

"There," she said, patting my shoulder so that I knew to sit down. "Much better."

I closed my eyes as Madame Colette began to brush my hair, but I couldn't shake the feeling that her forgiveness had come too easily. "Madame," I began. "You must let me apologize for the other day. I overstepped my bounds, and—"

She paused with the brush still in my hair.

"Overstepped your bounds?" she repeated. "No, dear girl, that is something that you could never do. Not as long as Monsieur Henri and I reside at Rousseau Manor. I need to tell you—"

There was a long silence that followed. I held my breath, wondering what Madame Colette was going to say.

"I am sure you have already heard about our daughter, Claudia," she continued quietly. "The light of our lives. The hope of our hearts. From the moment she was born, Claudia was everything to us, and we adored her."

I sat very still.

"And yet when she was nearly grown, there came a horrible night when the three of us argued, as even the most loving families sometimes do. When Henri and I awoke in the morning, we discovered to our eternal regret that our dear Claudia had left us. It's funny. I had always hoped that my only child would be courageous enough to follow her heart, and yet when she finally did, I found myself quite unprepared to handle it."

"Did she ever come back?" I dared to ask. "Where

is Mademoiselle Claudia now?"

"She died," Madame Colette said sadly. "She died, and not a day goes by that I don't miss her terribly."

It was just as I had feared, and yet somehow the news was even harder to bear when I heard Madame Colette say it aloud.

"I'm so sorry," I breathed. "I wish I could have met her."

"So do I, my dear," Madame Colette replied, her voice quivering. "So do I."

I twisted around to look at her and saw two tears spill down her cheeks. *Now I've done it again,* I thought miserably. *I've made Madame Colette cry.* How could I make her feel better? I was unexpectedly tempted to tell her all about Mademoiselle Claudia's diary, safely hidden in the mattress. If Madame Colette didn't know it existed, she would surely be thrilled to have one more connection with her daughter.

But what if she suspected me of reading it? Or even worse—what if the diary only served to upset her more? No, I couldn't tell her. The risk was too great.

"Here," Madame Colette said suddenly as she pressed her hairbrush into my hand. "This is for you."

**11**

$\mathcal{U}$nder normal circumstances, the servants at Rousseau Manor were so busy that the hours passed by in a blink. But as we waited for the Rousseaus to return, the day seemed to drag, each minute stretching out longer than the one before. The entire staff, from Bernadette and Mrs. Plourde to Agnès in the scullery, could talk of nothing but the imminent arrival of Mademoiselle Claire.

In hopes of passing the time, I pushed Baby Sophie in her pram around the grounds. Orchard, lily pond, fountain. Orchard, lily pond, fountain. But not even the darting dragonflies or the nest of baby robins could distract me today. All I could think about was Mademoiselle Claire, approaching closer with every passing minute. What would she be like? Tall or short, loud or quiet, happy or serious, kind or cruel? It seemed impossible to wait one minute more to meet

Madame Colette's fine silver hairbrush—belonging to a simple servant girl like me? That was unthinkable! Then I took a closer look at the hairbrush and realized, to my surprise, that it wasn't Madame Colette's at all.

Instead, it was Mademoiselle Claudia's hairbrush—the same one that I had so carefully polished for Mademoiselle Claire. I recognized the wreath of forget-me-nots circling the letter $C$ at once.

"No," I exclaimed, trying to give it back to Madame Colette. "I mustn't. It's not right."

"I want you to have it," she insisted. "And I am sure that Claudia would have, as well. You see—"

"There is my busy little bumblebee!" Monsieur Henri's voice rang out as he entered the room. Madame Colette quickly twisted around in her chair, dabbing her eyes so that he would not see her tears.

I stood up and curtsied to Monsieur Henri.

"Look at me. Just look," he said to Madame Colette, patting his stomach. "I have grown fat with no one to help me eat cookies at lunch. I know I was a grumpy old bear, but I hope that my little bee will not stay away any longer. Do you think that she will forgive me?"

I smiled up at him as I nodded enthusiastically.

"A capacity for forgiveness is just one of Camille's many fine qualities," Madame Colette said brightly. All traces of her tears were gone.

"Tomorrow we bring Claire here, to her new home," Monsieur Henri said to me. "I know that we can count on you to make her feel welcome."

"It would be an honor," I replied.

"It is not right for a house to sit silent and stuffy, puffed up with its own importance," Monsieur Henri declared. "A house needs children in it—especially a house like Rousseau Manor."

"I daresay that Rousseau Manor will soon be ringing with children's laughter, up and down every corridor," Madame Colette said. "Tell me, Camille, how are Bernadette's little cousins? Sophie and . . ."

"Alexandre," I said. "I like them. Sophie is sweet as sugar. I very much enjoy my time with her."

"Excellent," Monsieur Henri said. "And the boy? Is he good and kind? I know he is a hard worker—I have seen him through the window, day in, day out, toiling in the gardens alongside his father."

*Where once the topiaries grew,* I thought sadly. But all I said was, "Yes. He seems good and kind."

"I am glad to hear it," Monsieur Henri said. "Now, little bumblebee, I must finish preparing for our trip to the train station tomorrow. But when I return, we will dine together at lunch, yes?"

"Yes," I said happily. "Good night, Monsieur Henri. Good night, Madame Colette."

I stepped outside onto the landing and closed the door behind me, feeling happier and lighter than I had in days.

Changes were coming to Rousseau Manor.

And I could hardly wait for them!

her. I sighed as my frustration got the better of me.

"What's wrong, Camille?" someone said.

I turned around to see Alexandre standing behind me, holding his cap in his hands. He reached into the pram to tickle Sophie under her chin.

"Good morning, Alexandre," I said with a smile. "You mustn't mind me. I'm afraid I've grown quite impatient waiting for Mademoiselle Claire to arrive."

"Oh," he replied. "Yes, everyone's making quite a fuss over her, and she isn't even here yet."

"Well, it's not every day that an American orphan comes to live at Rousseau Manor," I said.

"True . . . but there are other interesting things happening here," Alexandre said mysteriously.

I eyed him curiously. "Like what?" I couldn't help asking.

Alexandre's whole face lit up. "Want to see?" he asked eagerly.

I knew right away what he wanted to show me: the new garden that he and his father had planted in place of the topiaries. Alexandre meant well, I was sure, but I still didn't feel ready to see the change. But he looked so excited that I couldn't refuse him.

*The topiaries aren't coming back,* I told myself. *Might as well get it over with.*

"All right," I said, trying to sound cheerful about it.

Sure enough, Alexandre led me in the direction of the topiary garden, chattering all the while. I'm ashamed to admit it, but my mind started to wander as thoughts of Mademoiselle Claire filled my head.

Alexandre tugged my arm, jolting me back to reality. "Well?" he said, and I had the sudden feeling that he was repeating himself. "What do you think?"

"Very n—" I started to say. But what I saw before me left me speechless. I pressed my hand to my heart. "Oh, Alexandre," I whispered. "How—"

Alexandre's smile stretched even broader as we stood side by side, looking up at a majestic pair of swans that had been sculpted from a boxwood bush. Their necks were twined together in the shape of a heart—just the way I remembered from when Papa was the groundskeeper. There was a freshly planted rosebush at the base of the topiary.

"We weren't sure we could do it," Alexandre was saying. "My father said he didn't know how, and neither one of us is much of an artist anyway, but then—then—then I found this, when we were cleaning out the shed—"

Alexandre reached into his back pocket and pulled out a slim volume. I reached for it cautiously, already overcome by emotion. I had a feeling that the book was something very special.

"This is Papa's handwriting," I whispered. Every page was covered with it—lines and lines of notes about each topiary animal, with sketches that he'd drawn with his very own hand!

"My father was impressed," Alexandre said, gesturing at the book. "He said your papa was a good groundskeeper. A talented one. He left such good instructions behind that we thought we'd give it a go. The swans to start . . . then the monkeys . . . then the elephant. I think we'll leave the peacock for last, though Father went ahead and ordered the morning glory seeds already."

"It's going to be beautiful," I said, my voice trembling with gratitude. "It already is. What a way to welcome Mademoiselle Claire!"

Alexandre looked at me blankly. "That's not—" he began to say.

But I kept talking. "I think that she will be so charmed by the topiary garden," I told him. "When she is sad, or lonesome, or homesick, she can come sit among the animals and be cheered by them." I sat down in the grass beside the swans and breathed in deeply; the rich perfume of the roses filled the air. *Yes,* I thought, *Mademoiselle Claire will like it here.*

"This was very kind of you," I said, looking up at Alexandre with a grateful smile. "*You* know what she's going through . . . leaving your home and coming to Rousseau Manor a veritable stranger. Of course, you already knew your papa's cousin, so I imagine that made it a bit less frightening—"

Alexandre seemed even more confused. "My papa's cousin?" he repeated. "Who?"

"Why, Bernadette, of course," I replied.

Alexandre shook his head. "Bernadette is no relation to us," he said. "We met her only last month."

Now it was my turn to be confused. "What did you say?" I asked.

"We were still living in the church," Alexandre said in a quiet voice. "She came up to my parents and asked Father if he knew anything about gardening.

She said she knew of a fine estate in need of a perma-
nent groundskeeper. Of course, Father jumped at the
opportunity. He'd been out of work for such a long
time, and we had no place to live. . . ."

"I'm sorry, Alexandre. That's terrible," I said.
"However it came to be, I'm very glad that Bernadette
brought you here."

But inside my thoughts were swirling. Hadn't
Bernadette insisted that Pierre was her cousin? Could
it be that Alexandre didn't know that she was a rela-
tive? No, that didn't make any sense at all. There was
only one explanation: Bernadette had lied.

But why?

*It was the goodness of her heart,* I thought suddenly.
Somehow Bernadette, who seemed so skilled at cruelty
and unkindness, had discovered Alexandre's family
in need. Knowing all too well that Rousseau Manor
was filled to capacity, she had come up with a plan
to ensure that Madame Colette would allow them to
come here—even though it had required her to lie to
her employers, an offense that could cause her to lose
her job if it were ever discovered.

*I've misjudged her,* I realized. Because anyone who

was capable of taking a risk like that—and all for the benefit of strangers—could never scheme against me as I had feared.

"I have to go," I said, pushing myself up from the ground. As I did, though, a flash of light caught my eye. There was something—something shiny—half buried in the freshly turned dirt near the base of the rosebush.

I reached out curiously and brushed the dirt away. There it was—an old silver coin, tarnished but still bright, just waiting to be discovered. I held my breath as I polished it with my apron.

"Is this yours?" I asked Alexandre, but he shook his head.

"I've never seen it before," he replied. "Maybe it was buried in the dirt and we dug it up when we planted the rosebush."

"It's quite peculiar," I continued as I took a closer look. One side looked like a regular coin, with writing on it in a language that I didn't recognize. The other side had been engraved with an image of two swans. And there was something else etched on it too.

"What do you make of that?" I asked Alexandre, who squinted at the coin.

"Looks like letters to me," he said. "Initials, perhaps?"

"An *H*...and a *B*?" I guessed. I tried to remember if I knew anyone at Rousseau Manor with those initials, but my mind was blank. I pressed the coin into my palm. The cool weight of it felt, somehow, familiar and comforting in my hand. It felt like it belonged there.

"When Mademoiselle Claire arrives, we'll all gather out front to welcome her," I told Alexandre. "I'll see you there."

"Where are you going?" he called after me, but I was already pushing Sophie's pram as fast as I could.

"There's something I have to do," I called back to him as we rounded a bend in the path.

Inside Rousseau Manor, I found Bernadette right where I expected: poring over the household accounts ledger in her office.

"Pardon the interruption," I said breathlessly as I shifted a very wiggly Sophie to my other hip.

Bernadette's mouth twisted in displeasure when she saw me. "What do you want?" she asked bluntly.

I took a step toward her desk and lowered my voice. "I know the truth about the Archambault family," I said. "I know they're not related to you."

A look of panic careened across Bernadette's face. She fairly flew across the room to shut the door.

"Camille—" she began urgently. But I wouldn't let her finish.

"And I just want to tell you that I think that's one of the bravest, most beautiful things I've ever heard," I continued. "To think of everything you risked to bring them here—and all to give a home to a homeless family."

Bernadette blinked a few times as if she didn't understand a word I was saying. *The shock, of course,* I thought. *And she must be afraid now that her secret is known.* Just then Sophie rested her little head on my shoulder, and I knew what I had to do.

"Anyway, you needn't worry about me," I promised Bernadette. "I'll never tell a soul, not even Mama."

At last Bernadette found her voice. "Th-th-thank you, Camille," she said. Her eyes were watery, almost like they were filled with tears, so I gave her a reassuring smile.

"I hope that when the time comes for me to be as brave and as selfless as you, I'll rise to the occasion," I told her.

Bernadette looked as though there were something else she wanted to say, but at that moment one of the servants threw open the door without even knocking. Normally such an infraction would earn a tongue-lashing from Bernadette, but we knew right away what had happened.

"The carriage approaches!" the servant cried, her face shining with glee.

Bernadette and I dashed out after her, nearly running headfirst into Élise, who had come to fetch Sophie. There was a great clatter and commotion throughout the halls as the kitchen staff changed into their nicest aprons and the housemaids adjusted their lace-trimmed caps. In mere moments, we were assembled—all thirty of us—in a straight line out front. Even Rousseau Manor seemed to be waiting with us.

Mama gave one last attempt at my hair, tucking a few stray strands behind my ears. I glanced down the long line and saw Alexandre standing with his family. He waved at me, which made me grin. Already I couldn't imagine Rousseau Manor without the Archambaults.

Then I heard it: the carriage wheels rattling over the

road and the loud *clop-clop-clop* of the horses' hooves. My heart started pounding. I reached into my pocket for the unusual coin I'd found in the topiary garden. Just holding it made me feel calmer. Stronger. Ready— for whatever would happen next.

After the coachman stopped the carriage directly in front of Rousseau Manor, he opened the door. Madame Colette appeared first, followed by Monsieur Henri; then they held out their hands to help her out of the carriage.

Mademoiselle Claire.

She was here at last.

I craned my neck, trying to get a better look at her as the introductions began—until Mama nudged me, a reminder of the proper way to stand at attention. I stared straight ahead, finding patience I didn't know I had.

Then Monsieur Henri and Madame Colette were standing before me. "And this, Claire, is Camille LeClerc," Madame Colette said in her gentlest voice.

I dropped into such a deep curtsy that my knee grazed the ground. "Welcome, Mademoiselle Claire," I said, staring at the toes of her beautiful satin shoes. "It is an honor to serve you."

Then, to my surprise, I felt a hand on my elbow, pulling me up.

It was Mademoiselle Claire herself! We stood facing each other, and I saw her—really saw her—for the first time: her beautiful skin, as fair and freckle-free as a pitcher of cream; her dark, wavy hair, arranged in a stylish bob; her pale green eyes, as full of anxiety and anticipation as my own heart. She looked as though she wanted to smile, if only she could remember how. So I smiled at her instead. Then, suddenly, she embraced me—me, a servant girl! And as we hugged—it's so hard to describe, but somehow I felt as though I had always known her, had always been waiting for this moment.

"Please," she said. "Call me Claire."

*Every*
*Secrets of the Manor*
*story leads to another.*

**Read on for a first look at**
Claire's Story,
1910

$\mathcal{C}$ome now, my dear Claire," Cousin Colette said. "You must be exhausted from your journey. I'm sure you would appreciate some quiet time to rest in your new room."

I nodded my head in agreement, but to be honest, I didn't feel a bit tired—not one bit! I was far too jumpy and jangly with anticipation, and what I really wanted to do was explore every inch of Rousseau Manor's grand house and grounds. I wanted to spend hours getting to know my cousins Henri and Colette Rousseau, who would be my guardians from now on. Most of all, I wanted to do everything I could to make this unfamiliar place feel like home—and to make these strangers feel like family.

The best way to do that, it seemed, was to do exactly what my new guardians asked of me. That's why I didn't resist when Cousin Colette and Cousin Henri led me past the receiving line of servants and through the entrance of Rousseau Manor. But I did turn my head around to peek behind me one more time. The girl near the end of the line was still standing there, watching me—Camille, she was called—and as soon as our eyes met, she smiled. I smiled back as I waved at her over my shoulder. We were almost the exact same height, which made me think Camille was nearly twelve years old, like me. She was the very first person my age I'd met since I had arrived in Paris. There was something about her—a spark of kindness, I think, or maybe it was the friendly way her face crinkled up when she smiled—that made me wish we could be friends. But Camille was a servant here, and I had no idea when I'd see her again.

"This way, Claire." Cousin Colette's voice interrupted my thoughts.

She stepped over to the butler for a brief word and then returned to my side. "We've chosen a room on the second floor of the East Wing for you," she said as we climbed the spiral staircase. "I hope that you'll find the room suitable. With the eastern exposure, you'll have a lovely view of the sunrise each morning. Of course, you may not be an early riser, but I can assure you the curtains are velvet and very thick; they'll be sure to block out the light. And if there is anything about the decor you'd like to change, you need only say the word. . . ."

Cousin Colette's voice trailed off as she reached out to open the door. I caught a quick glimpse of a canopy bed with billowing white curtains, blue velvet drapes, and a plush rug to match, but I didn't need to see my new room to express my gratitude.

"It's perfect," I said. "Thank you."

A relieved smile washed over Cousin Colette's face, and for the first time I wondered if she felt as nervous as I did. She squeezed my hand as the footmen arrived, bearing my trunks.

"Where would you like them, Mademoiselle Claire?" the taller one asked.

"Oh, anywhere is fine," I said. "Perhaps by the window?" It had a deep window seat that was crowded with velvet pillows; I could already tell that I would spend many happy hours there, basking in the morning sun as I read my favorite books.

"You mustn't worry about the unpacking," Cousin Henri said. "The entire staff here is at your service and will be more than happy to assist you in any way they can."

"Thank you," I repeated. Perhaps I should've told them that unpacking as quickly as possible was all part of my plan to make Rousseau Manor feel like home. But I didn't quite know how to say it, so we stood together in an uncomfortable silence, the way strangers might stand together on the platform as they await the next train.

Suddenly, Cousin Colette leaned forward to embrace me. "We are so glad you have come to Rousseau Manor," she whispered near my ear, "though we wish it had happened under different circumstances."

Tears pricked at my eyes then, but I tried to blink them away. There would be no melancholy or weepy moments for me. No, I would be happy and cheerful and a joy to have at Rousseau Manor. That was the vow I had made on the voyage from America. After all, that's what Mother and Father would've wanted me to do.

But were those tears shining in Cousin Colette's eyes as well? I knew what it looked like when adults were trying not to cry in front of me. I'd seen it quite a bit in the last few weeks.

"We'll send Bernadette in later on to help you dress for dinner," she finished.

Cousin Henri smiled winningly at me before he escorted Cousin Colette from the room.

And then I was all alone for perhaps the first time since the accident that had killed my parents and left me an orphan. Since that terrible night, everyone had been so tremendously *kind* to me . . . and the people of Rousseau Manor were no exception.

I went straight to my trunk and unlatched the strong brass buckles. I didn't even notice how anxious I was until I eased open the lid, waiting to see if the precious contents had survived the rough crossing overseas. My hands were trembling a bit as I unwrapped the bundles—the big one first. I opened the sturdy case and breathed a sigh of relief to discover that Father's beautiful violin was in perfect condition, looking just as it had the very last time he had played for me. The polished wood gleamed in a beam of sunlight as I lightly rested my fingers on the taut strings. After I unpacked the bow, perhaps I could play a little. If I closed my eyes, it might even feel like Father was playing for me once more.

I reached for the second bundle, which was much smaller and lighter. Inside the silk handkerchief, I found them: Mother's favorite pair of gloves and a small cameo brooch that she always wore pinned to the front of her dress.

I slipped my hands into the gloves, knowing that hers were the last hands to wear them. They even smelled like her delicate perfume. A wide smile filled my face; anywhere would feel like home with these special reminders of Mother and Father by my side.

I reached into the trunk for Father's bow and found something surprising instead:

A letter.

*I don't remember any letters in here when the maids helped me pack my trunk,* I thought as a confused frown spread across my face. But sure enough, my name was written on the front in perfect, elegant script. I opened the envelope and began to read.

*Dear Claire,*

*As I write this letter on the eve of*

your departure, there is much hope swirling through my heart: that you will have a pleasant journey; that you will find France to be as wonderful and welcoming as I have during my visits; that you will feel quite at home the moment you arrive at Rousseau Manor; and, most of all, that the grief you feel for your parents will be replaced by only the sweetest memories of them.

You know, of course, that your mother was a dear friend, and her untimely passing is a great injustice that no one who loved her should have to bear. And yet I have found that your presence here at Vandermeer Manor has done wonders to soothe my grief. It is a testament to your character, Claire, that even in the face of such tragedy, you are compassionate and kind. More than once

I have observed you at play with Kate and little Alfie and thought about how proud your parents would be of your strength and resiliency.

Knowing this, I am confident that you will find a warm welcome at Rousseau Manor and soon feel very much at home there. I met Henri and Claudia many years ago and found them to be a charming couple with generous, giving hearts. And when you find yourself on American shores once more, I do hope you will visit us here at Vandermeer Manor. We will always have a room ready for you, and I look forward to seeing your sweet face at my table once more.

With my fondest regards,

Mrs. Katherine Vandermeer

I read the letter twice more before I finally returned it to its envelope. It was just like dear, sweet Mrs. Vandermeer, Kate and Alfie's great-grandmother, to write something so kind and heartening, then slip it into my trunk so that I should discover it right when I might need some reassurance! Reading her words made me wish, for the briefest moment, that I was still at Vandermeer Manor, listening to Kate practice her reading or helping Alfie arrange his toy soldiers. A wave of homesickness washed over me as I sat beside my trunk, all alone in a strange land.

A sudden knock at the door interrupted my thoughts.

"Come in," I said, scrambling to my feet as I hurried to take off Mother's gloves. I'd thought it would be Cousin Colette, or perhaps a housemaid to help me unpack, but instead it was the girl I'd met in the receiving line. Camille.

"Pardon the interruption, Mademoiselle Claire," she said right away, ducking into a curtsy as she balanced a heavy tray, "but we thought that you might be in need of some refreshments."

"What's this?" I cried as I hurried across the room.

The tray was so laden with treats that I marveled at Camille's ability to carry it, let alone curtsy without spilling a single thing. There were slices of crusty bread and a wedge of creamy cheese; a basket filled to the brim with cookies; a platter of pastries; a bowl of chocolate-covered strawberries; and a tall glass of milk. There was even a vase filled with a large, fragrant white flower.

"How beautiful!" I gasped as I leaned down to sniff it. I didn't remember the name of the flower, but its scent reminded me of Mother. She'd grown flowers like this in one of our gardens.

"Where did you get this?" I asked Camille, hardly daring to hope that other flowers like this one might grow somewhere on the grounds of Rousseau Manor.

"It comes from the flower garden," she told me. "Tomorrow, if you'd like, I would be happy to give you a tour of the house and grounds."

"Would you really?" I asked in excitement. "That would be wonderful. Thank you!"

"It would be my pleasure, Mademoiselle Claire. I will come to your room after breakfast."

"Please, you really must call me Claire," I told her.

Camille looked a bit worried. "Are you—are you sure?" she asked. "It seems so informal . . . disrespectful, almost. . . ."

"Nonsense!" I replied. Then, impulsively, I gestured toward the window seat. "Come. You must join me. I can't eat *all* of this by myself!"

I closed the lid of my trunk so that it became a table for us. "What should I try first?" I asked.

Camille looked at the tray thoughtfully. "Well, these are my favorites," she said, pointing at a puffed-up ball of pastry with a thin glaze of chocolate on top. "They're called profiteroles, and they're filled with custard."

"Mmm," I said as I reached for one and took a bite. "Delicious!"

Camille smiled so proudly that I wondered if she had made them. I was about to ask when she suddenly said, "A violin!"

"It belonged to my father," I explained.

A look of understanding flashed through Camille's eyes. "What a special thing to have," she said as she squeezed my hand. "My papa died when I was five years old, and Mama let me keep one of his red handkerchiefs. I still have it."

*She knows,* I thought as I smiled gratefully at Camille. *She knows what this feels like.*

"Do you play?" she continued.

"Oh, no," I said, shaking my head. "Well, a little, I suppose. But badly—very badly. I only wish I had inherited my father's musical gifts!"

Camille giggled. "I feel the same way about my mother's culinary skills," she confided. "She's a genius in the kitchen, but I'm a laughingstock, an absolute disaster!"

She turned away briefly to glance at the clock hanging on the wall.

"I really must go, I'm afraid," she said as she rose. "I need to watch Baby Sophie while her mother prepares the servants' meal."

I rose with her. "Thank you for the visit and the refreshments," I replied, though what I wanted to say was, *I do wish you could stay!*

After Camille took her leave, my new room seemed so much quieter and lonesome. *Perhaps I should've insisted that she stay,* I thought. But of course I would never do such a thing—not when she had responsibilities to attend to. It would be unfair to put her in such a position.

*There's no reason I can't start exploring the gardens myself,* I decided. I put on my favorite hat, the one with embroidered cherries scattered around the brim, and reached for my smart spring coat. Just before I left my room, I decided to take Father's violin with me. He always loved to play outdoors on a bright spring day or a warm summer evening. Perhaps I would grow to love it, too.

Outside, I followed a stone path around the back of the house, where the gardens stretched out like a beautiful patchwork quilt. A tall hedge lined the path, which twisted and turned across the property. I followed it until I came to a lovely little garden that was positively bursting with flowers in bloom, including the ones that Mother used to grow! How I wished I could remember the name of those flowers.

There was a white marble bench in the middle of the garden, so I sat on it while I removed Father's violin from the case and added a little extra rosin to the bow. Then, after carefully positioning my chin on the leather chin rest, I began to play his favorite song from memory. But the notes sounded all wrong! It was no secret that I was a poor excuse for a musician, especially compared to Father; I stopped playing after a screechy note that was off-tempo besides. The last thing I wanted to do was butcher Father's favorite song.

Then I tried my hand at a simpler tune. It wasn't anything special, but I played it passably well. I closed my eyes as I imagined what he would say if he could hear my playing: "Better. Better! I can tell you've been practicing!" Even though we both knew that I hadn't been—not as much as I should've, anyway.

The memory brought a smile to my face, but it lasted only a moment before it faded. I had the strangest sense . . . a creeping feeling that started at the base of my head before crawling down my spine. It felt like someone was *watching* me.

I opened my eyes. "Who's there?" I called out loudly. Half the battle in facing one's fears was to face them head-on, or at least, that's what Mother always used to tell me. So I was pleasantly surprised by how steady my voice sounded.

I listened carefully but heard no reply. I had no

choice but to conclude that I was alone in the little garden: completely, totally, and utterly alone.

Yet the feeling persisted; if anything, it grew stronger, until I was as certain as I could be that no matter what my eyes told me, I was not by myself after all.

I didn't dare hope that I might be feeling the presence of my dear father visiting me from the world beyond. I would be twelve years old in a few months, and everyone knew that twelve was way too grown-up to believe in specters and haunts from beyond the grave.

Even though I would've given anything—*anything*—for one more afternoon with my parents.

I took a deep breath and nestled Father's violin under my chin once more. Then, taking extra care to hold the bow just so and to place my fingers firmly against the strings, I again attempted to play Father's favorite song . . . just in case.